Jan's Journey

"I think you need therapy too," said Claire, looking straight at him.

He stood up suddenly, roughly pushing the chair away. "Why do you think this?" he demanded. "You think I am a nutter just because I don't take you to supper?"

"I didn't say that." Claire glared at him. "I mean, just look at you – you're stressed out right now!"

There was a moment's pause. They faced each other over the table, dark eyes blazing into grey, both faces white with anger, overlaying other emotions – concern in Claire, fear in Jan.

Suddenly he spoke. "Stressed? *Maybe*." He got the word right for once. "But who is stressing me?" he asked.

He turned abruptly and left the room.

Also available:

Katie Goes to College
Claire's Conquests

Look out for:

Nikki's New World

Point

NURSES

Jan's Journey

Bette Paul

SCHOLASTIC

Scholastic Children's Books
Commonwealth House, 1–19 New Oxford Street,
London WC1A 1NU
a division of Scholastic Ltd
London ~ New York ~ Toronto ~ Sydney ~ Auckland

First published by Scholastic Ltd, 1996

ISBN 0 590 13348 9

Typeset by TW Typesetting, Midsomer Norton, Avon

Printed by Cox & Wyman Ltd, Reading, Berks.

10 9 8 7 6 5 4 3 2 1

Prologue

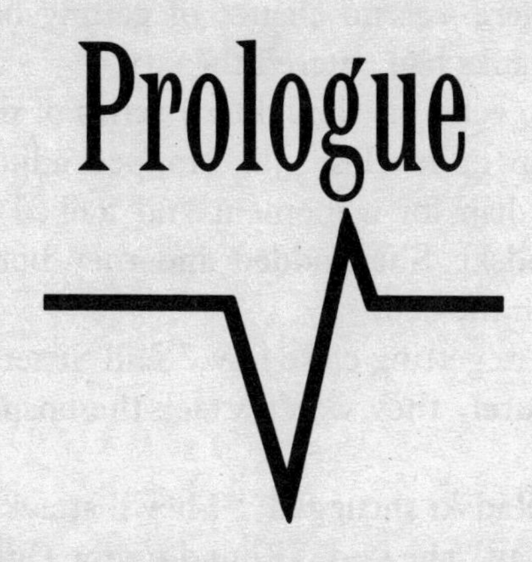

Everyone clamoured for attention.

"Water – for the love of God a drink of water!"

"Bring me a bed-pan – quick!"

"The blood's seeping through. More bandage, please."

"Something for the pain, please, Doctor."

Jan Buczowski smiled grimly to himself; it was nice to be addressed as "doctor" even though he was only a medical orderly. His smile faded as he remembered the real doctor of the family – his mother. She'd always wanted him to follow her profession and he'd always resisted. Well, she'd be proud of him now, wherever she was. But where *was* she now? And his father? Not in conference with some government committee these days, surely.

Across the river at home with Granya, he fervently hoped, though they might as well be on a different planet; there was no chance of getting back there now the tanks had entered the city.

As if to echo his thoughts, a series of dull thuds started up quite close. Jan stopped adjusting the patient's drip for a moment and looked across at Sister Radski. She nodded and they both moved away from the bed.

"They're getting close now," said Sister.

"But surely they won't attack the hospital?" Jan protested.

Sister Radski shrugged. "They'll attack anything in their way," she said. "Round up the children and take them down to the basement."

"What about these people?" Jan looked around the ward, where everyone was badly wounded, immobilized.

"I'll wheel them across to the inside wall, well away from the windows."

"And you?" he asked anxiously. Tanya Radski had been a good friend to him – and a good teacher; what little he knew of nursing came from her. They'd been on duty together on and off – mostly on – for over a week now and Jan had learned to admire the tough little Sister.

Through the dust and grime on her face, and the exhaustion in her eyes, Tanya smiled. "I'll stay here – well away from the windows, don't you worry."

But Jan did worry. As he heaved injured children down the flights of narrow steps, along the sand-bagged passages and into the candle-lit store rooms deep under the hospital building, he wondered how Tanya was getting on.

I'll go back and help her, he decided, just as soon as I've finished here.

But as soon as he'd got the children to safety, the adult patients were on their way. They lined the stairwell, supporting each other, two, sometimes three abreast. Jan knew he couldn't leave them there; he stood at the bottom of the steps, lifting, heaving, pushing them in through the door to the basement, like so many hunks of meat.

And all the time he was aware of the dull, heavy thud of gunfire and, he realized, the steady rumble of traffic. The tanks were coming up the hospital drive! Even then he couldn't make himself believe they would fire on the hospital; not until he pushed his way up to the ground floor to help a couple of walking wounded down. There, he was almost knocked down as a dozen soldiers stampeded through the foyer, hauling machine guns, clutching rifles, thrusting aside anyone unlucky enough to be in their way. Jan's heart sank. Snipers! They'd be off to the top floor to fire on anything that moved outside. They'd been sent to defend the hospital, but what could they do against armoured tanks? Only stir them into action, Jan realized with a shudder.

And he was right. Soon after, he was ushering another batch of patients to the top of the steps to the basement when there came a thud so loud it hurt the back of his ears. Then silence – for whole minutes it seemed – followed by a kind of slithering groan as the front of the building collapsed. Jan felt the floor shudder and settle under his feet.

"Go on – move!" he commanded, shoving the patients down the steps so that they stumbled into the crowd. And even as they moved, he heard the shattering of glass as the ground-floor windows began to splinter into the foyer.

Now the narrow concrete stairway was crowded with people. No one waited for his help – they crawled, hobbled, staggered, some on one foot, a few lucky ones with crutches; others sitting, bobbing from step to step like babies, they surged downwards like a living stream while Jan stood helpless at the top of the stairs, watching them flounder like so many fish in a net.

He should be down there with them, he thought, to help sort them out. But how could he? Peering down through the dim, dusty light he could see a solid mass of bodies jammed into the narrow passage. He had no idea how many people were already down there; he didn't even know how far the basement reached underground. He'd worked up on the first floor ever since he'd reported to the hospital when the university was blown up. All students, male and female, had been ordered into the army, but those with even the slightest medical training were sent to the hospitals. Biology was Jan's subject – not much use when it came to dealing with broken limbs and shrapnel wounds, he knew, but somewhat safer than guerrilla warfare up in the hills.

Until now. Jan felt the floor shift beneath him and, looking up, saw the jagged edges of cracks appearing up the walls. Another thud and the staircase seemed to lean slightly, the cracks grew wider, and the metal handrail twisted like a live thing as people struggled to hold on to it. The whole building above them seemed to groan then settle, like an old lady on a sofa.

If it falls we'll all be trapped, thought Jan, and he took a step back. Maybe it was safer up here? For a moment he thought of making a run for it – out the back, anywhere away from the sound of gunfire, rifle shots, screaming and howling as whole wards collapsed above him. But he couldn't leave all those people down there. Could he? Jan hesitated.

Then a voice boomed across the remains of the foyer.

"All medical staff report to the ground floor – urgent – all medical staff this way…"

Jan couldn't believe his luck; it was as if he'd asked permission to leave and it had been granted.

"Hey, get a move on!" Somebody rushed past.

"You're medical, aren't you? You're needed out at the back."

Jan almost leapt to attention and, turning his back on the sight and sound of the distressed, disabled people lining the staircase, he fled.

Within days there was no hospital left in Czerny. No electricity, no water, no food – almost no city. Medical help was reduced to mere first aid, nursing duties to comforting and smoothing brows. The remains of the hospital staff, and the few wounded, sick, and dying they tended, existed – it could not be called living – in the battered remains of a school, huddled in the dark rooms under desks and tables, eating an occasional dry biscuit and sipping water from burst mains.

"They're coming to get us out," a young half-qualified doctor told Jan one day. "UN troops are on their way."

And Jan was too exhausted even to ask why. Two days later his plane touched down somewhere in the east of England and he was given clean warm clothing, a cursory medical and a bed in a hut on an ex-RAF airfield. Jan Buczowski had a new home.

Chapter 1

Jan closed his eyes and gripped the arms of his seat as the plane wheels touched the tarmac. Next to him, Claire Donovan leaned over and put a comforting hand on his shoulder. Jan flinched away. He knew Claire was puzzled and hurt, but he could say nothing to reassure her, not while the black hole of panic filled his brain. Inwardly he cursed; why had it happened just then? He wasn't afraid of flying; had done the outward journey to Belfast calmly – eagerly, even – four days ago. All his life he'd accompanied his parents on flights – to medical conferences with his mother, Soviet universities with Dad... He cut off the memory.

"It's all right, we're landed," Claire was saying. And he knew he had to open his eyes.

"Yes," he breathed. "A tense moment."

"It always is." She smiled, reassuringly. "But we're down now, safe and sound."

"Safe and sound," he repeated. And he was; the blackness had receded, the thudding in his ears stopped, he was back on firm ground. "Terra firma," he muttered.

"What?" Claire looked at him, worried.

"Nothing." He laughed a little. "Now, shall we take the bus or the train into Brassington?"

"Taxi," said Claire firmly. "Da gave me the money, we may as well use it."

Jan nodded, though without enthusiasm. It would have been nice, just once, to have contributed something to the weekend's pleasures. And there had been so many at the Leonmohr Hotel, which Claire's parents owned: a beautiful room overlooking the bay, several sumptuous feasts, walks along the wide, deserted beaches, log fires to come home to – all without asking. And there was Claire, beside him all day and long into the evening when the two of them made music for the family and their friends. Jan couldn't remember when he'd last been so cosseted, so obviously cherished. And felt so guilty. He gave a huge sigh.

"Is that a sigh of relief you're feeling now we've landed?" Claire teased.

"And a little sadness now that the holiday's over," he replied – almost truthfully.

"Not for long; we'll have a wonderful time there at Christmas." Claire beamed up at him, obviously anticipating his acceptance.

"But first we must work, eh, Claire?" Jan fielded the answer to her invitation. It had been a wonderful holiday, but… "Ah! Doors open," he said with relief. "After you!"

They were carrying only hand luggage and so were very quickly on their way into the centre of Brassington and to its Royal Infirmary, known to medics and students alike as St Ag's.

"Will I do us a meal later?" asked Claire as the taxi pulled away from Kelham's, the nurses' home. "I've brought half the Leonmohr kitchen as usual."

Jan groaned. "After what I've eaten this weekend?" he joked. "No, really, I think I need a rest, Claire. The journey, you know."

"Yes, you don't look at all well." Claire looked anxiously into his face. "And I thought the fresh sea air would be good for you."

"Oh, it was marvellous," Jan assured her. "I just got a bit … a bit wheezy on the plane."

Claire looked puzzled. "Wheezy?" she asked.

He nodded. "Yes, you know – feeling a little sick."

"Ah – queasy – that's the word."

"Queasy," Jan repeated slowly, memorizing the new word as he always did. His English had improved rapidly with the help of The Six – his friends and colleagues at St Ag's – but there were hundreds of words still to learn, especially the colloquial, almost slangy words the others used so easily. "Queasy," he said again. "How do you spell that?"

He was still feeling queasy as he lay on his bed in his room. He'd take a little rest – a nap – and then go over to St Ag's to check his placement. The exam results would be out too, but he wasn't very interested in them – he knew he'd done well. Exams were no worry to Jan: he'd been well on with his biology degree before the civil war in his country. Chemistry, anatomy, biology – all the science subjects in the nursing course were elementary to him. It was the practicalities of nursing he found difficult. Not the blood, the vomit, the bed-pans – he'd seen all that and worse during the war back home. It was the patients, their attitude – whining, complaining, demanding. When he thought how brave his people had been, even with terrible wounds, horrendous burns, slow starvation… He sat up suddenly and opened his eyes wide. No! He didn't want to think of that.

"You're in Mental Health," Nick Bone told him. "And you've come top in the exams. Congratulations on both counts!"

"Thank you." Jan peered again at the notice

board in the common room. "Where did you see this – this Mental Health?"

"There." Nick pointed to the list. "They must think you had enough blood and gore on Men's Surgical last term."

"That I do not mind," said Jan.

"But nutters you do?" asked Nick cheerily.

"Nutters? What are they?"

"Ah, well." Knowing Jan's eagerness to extend his vocabulary, Nick hastily backtracked. "Not a word you'll need to know, Jan. Forget it."

Jan bowed his head slightly.

"You'll do well in Mental Health," Nick assured him. "A doddle after Surgical – and after exams."

"Exams – easy," Jan told him. "Surgical – interesting. But this Mental Health – this is not in the hospital, is it?"

Nick shook his head. "No, it's that new building across the grounds," he said. "Beautiful gardens and rooms with a view; treatment for healthy minds," he added, seeing Jan's uncomprehending expression.

"Healthy minds," Jan repeated. "But this is not medical?"

"Well, there are folk who'd tell you it's all in the mind," Nick smiled. "Healthy mind in a healthy body, you know?"

"*Mens sana in corpore sano*," Jan said softly.

"And you know Latin too!" Nick threw an arm

around Jan's shoulders. "Is there no end to your genius, young feller?"

Jan hastily moved away. "Ask me that at the end of term," he laughed, a little awkwardly.

"Oh, you'll enjoy Mental Health once you adjust," Nick assured Jan. "And once you relax," he added pointedly.

"But I am just back from relaxing," Jan protested.

"Ah, yes. Did you have a good time over at Claire's place?"

Jan blushed. "Certainly," he said stiffly. "It was very … luxurious." He pronounced the word carefully.

"You sound as if you disapprove," Nick observed.

"Everyone was very kind to me, very … careful. No – caring."

"A bit too caring, perhaps?"

"Can there be 'too caring'?" asked Jan, neatly avoiding the question that he'd asked himself all weekend.

"Oh, yes," Nick assured him. "Here's another little saying for your English notebook: 'smothering with kindness'."

"Smothering," Jan repeated the word perfectly. "But that is a way of killing, is it not?"

"It is," Nick agreed cheerfully. "Too much of it kills the spirit. A bit of healthy neglect is what we all need now and then." He stared hard at Jan. "See you!" he said, and breezed his way down the corridor.

Jan stood gazing vacantly after Nick, quietly repeating his words "a bit of healthy neglect". And he wasn't just practising his English: the phrase seemed to hold a special significance for him just then.

He suddenly remembered the exam list and looked along it to check the results of the rest of The Six, as the little group called themselves. He quickly scanned the computer print-out, which was in alphabetical order. Well, they'd all passed – Katie Harding with only a few marks less than himself, he noted. Even Claire's results were better than usual; she'd be relieved. Claire found the academic work very hard and relied on his help; revision sessions, finalizing course work, help with biology notes – Jan was on hand to help her through all of these. It was one of the things that had brought them together.

She might actually enjoy her period in college while he mouldered away in the non-medical world of Mental Health, he thought wryly. They were in different study modules; that was one of the things that kept them apart. Jan flushed, suddenly recognizing his feeling of relief. Of course, he told himself, he enjoyed being with Claire, was very grateful for the weekend he'd just spent with her family, loved making music with her, was perfectly willing to help her through the whole course if necessary. But...

Frowning, he thrust the "but" from his thoughts and made his way back to Kelham's.

Chapter 2

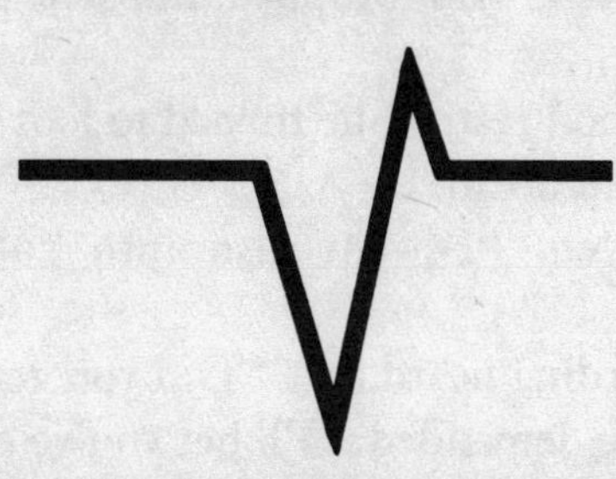

The sound of laughter drifted down the top corridor of Kelham's. It came from the kitchen, as did the pungent scent of spices. Barbara Robinson, not Claire, was providing the meal. Nevertheless, Jan walked cautiously past the kitchen door, hoping to go unseen.

"Hi, Jan! Come on in. Grandma's hot 'n' spicy pumpkin soup, all the way from sun-kissed Brixton," Barbara called through the part-open door.

"Thank you, but I'm not hungry." Jan popped his head into the kitchen, still hoping to make a quick getaway. "Not *very* hungry," he corrected himself as he watched Barbara pouring thick, golden liquid into bowls and saw the mounds of Irish soda bread on the table. Saw, too, Claire's face brighten as she turned to him. He went in.

"Irish-Caribbean cuisine today – yet another triumph for the talents of the Kelhamites!" Barbara handed him a bowl of soup. "Spoons on the table, chairs all taken, you'll have to prop up the worktop as usual."

So Jan went and propped himself up behind Claire.

"Had a good rest?" She turned to look up at him and offer him bread.

Jan nodded. "I went also into college," he admitted.

Katie Harding heard that. "Did you get the exam results?" she demanded. "I'll bet you've come top."

His mouth full of soda bread, Jan merely nodded.

"Does that mean you came top or you got the results?" teased Claire. She half-turned, looking up with shining eyes, and putting out a hand as if to touch him. Jan shuffled himself up on to the work-top, a little out of her reach.

"It means," he said, swallowing a lump of soda bread, "that I saw the results and..." He paused, rather enjoying the rapt attention of the girls. Even Barbara was wide-eyed.

"And?" she prompted.

"Well, I can tell you ... that..." Another pause.

"Get on with it, Jan! Don't be so tantalizing," begged Katie.

"Tanta- what?" asked Jan. "What does it mean?" He reached into his pocket for his notebook, but before he could find a pencil, Barbara had snatched the book away.

"You'll lose all your hard-won slang," she threatened, "if you don't tell us the results – now, immediately, *tout de suite*!"

Jan grinned. "Well, you've all passed," he said, holding out his hand for the notebook.

"Of course we have," said Barbara crossly. She slapped the book on to the table. "But what about the grades?"

Jan blushed. "I didn't much notice," he said. "The list was in the order of the alphabet."

"Come on, Jan," said Katie. "You're not telling me you don't even know your own grade?"

"Well, yes," he said carefully. "I do know that – and yours too, as a matter of fact."

"Then, as a matter of fact, tell me what I got!"

"Almost the same as I – we both passed Grade A."

"Yippeeee!" Katie Harding jumped up and thrust a clenched fist into the air.

"Well done, you two!" said Barbara, a little subdued.

"But you and Nick are also high – Grade B."

"Well, I expected at least that," said Barbara. "Nick Bone must be pleased with himself though," she added, a trifle patronizing. "What about the infants?" She often referred to Claire and Nikki in this way; although Katie was technically the youngest of them all, the other two had come into nursing straight from school.

Jan was uncomfortably aware of two pairs of anxious eyes still on him. He moved slightly so that he stood between Claire and Nikki Browne, placing a hand on each of their shoulders.

"Claire – a C. It's better than you expected, no?"

He felt her sigh of relief run right through his arm. "Oh, yes, thanks to you, love." She reached up and this time grasped his hand in hers. "Thank you," she said softly.

But Jan had already turned away to face Nikki.

"You too have passed," he said gently. There was no need to mention Nikki's grade, a basic pass – they all knew what he meant.

Nikki Brown gave a small, tight nod. "Thank you, Jan," was all she said.

There was a slightly awkward pause. Katie slid back into her seat, Barbara turned her attention to the stove and, for different reasons, Claire and Nikki sat staring at the wall in front of them.

"Well," said Jan. He put down his soup bowl. "After that succrumptious meal, I will wash up."

"Scrumptious or succulent," said Katie, "or even both, but not together."

The others laughed with relief. Now they were together again, not divided by their exam results.

"We must do something to celebrate," announced Katie.

"It'll have to be at the weekend," said Claire gloomily. "Have you seen our timetables for this module?"

Barbara and Katie groaned. They and Claire were in college for the next few weeks as they'd been on placement up to the exams. They went on talking together about schedules, seminars and tutorials, and Jan turned to Nikki.

"There is a list of placements too," he said. "But I am so sorry – I did not look for you."

Nikki looked round at him, like a startled rabbit. "Oh, that's all right; Sister Thomas told me before half-term."

Jan was surprised. Placements were supposed to be announced only a day ahead, to prevent too much agonizing and arguing. Which was just what he wanted to do with the idiot who'd put him on Mental Health, he reflected.

"Sister told you?" he asked.

And the others, catching his drift, turned their attention to Nikki.

"Why would she do that?" asked Katie.

Nikki shrugged. "She wanted me to be prepared, I suppose," she said.

"Why?" asked Katie, never one for subtlety.

Nikki took a deep breath, then paused. "I'm in the hospice," she said quietly.

"Wheeeew!" Katie whistled.

The others looked at Nikki with interest.

"You think you can face it?" asked Barbara.

"Well, you see..." Nikki hesitated, as she usually did before speaking. "That's why Sister Thomas told me – to give me time to prepare myself. Of course," she went on hurriedly in her clipped, well-bred voice, "there's no need to suppose anyone will actually – er – *go* while I'm there." It was obvious she was repeating Sister Thomas's words of comfort. "And anyway..." she went on, then stopped.

"Anyway?" Katie pressed her.

Nikki flushed and looked down at the table as if it was suddenly very interesting. "What is it people say – 'been there, done that'? I have faced the problem before, you know."

Another silence. It occurred to Jan that they knew very little about Nikki Browne. She was always rushing off home at every opportunity – weekends, free days – hence, he supposed, her poor exam results. But she never offered any explanation – merely turned down most of their invitations for weekend treats – film, disco, club – apologizing profusely and muttering about being needed at home.

"You will have a very interesting experience," said Jan seriously. "There is much courage in such a place."

Nikki brightened. "Is that what you found in the war in your country?" she asked.

Jan nodded. "Of course things were so fast; many

woundeds came and moved on, so we never knew what had become of them all. But some stayed and some died…" He closed his eyes, pushed the memory from him. "You will learn much at the hospice," he said.

"I hope so," said Nikki. "And where are they sending you this term?"

Jan grimaced. "I think maybe Sister Thomas should tell me before," he said. "Then I can change it."

"Why? Where are you going?" asked Claire.

"Maternity?" giggled Katie.

"Gynae?" added Barbara.

"Urology?" Nikki suggested.

Everyone laughed; these were all departments where most male nurses would rather not boldly go.

Jan shook his head. "Mental Health," he announced in hollow tones. He groaned and rubbed his hands through his hair nervously.

"Well, why all the fuss? It's great," said Barbara. "We did a visit there last term. No dressings, no drips, no messy beds, not even any wards. All the heavy work's done by domestic staff and the patients look after themselves. It's a doddle, man!"

"And it's a beautiful place," Nikki assured him. "I often walk through the woods down there – so peaceful."

"And Geoff Huckthwaite – the Charge Nurse –

he's a great bloke," said Katie. "Don't you remember him in the cabaret last summer? Killingly funny..."

They all smiled at the memory of the stocky ex-miner doing a drag act. Except for Jan; he couldn't find it in himself to smile at the prospect of six weeks in Mental Health, no matter how amusing the Charge Nurse was.

"Myself, I'm not pleased with this arrangement." He turned to open the door. "I shall go now and discuss with Sister Thomas. Goodbye, ladies!" He gave a mock bow and left.

"Oh, Jan – don't go! Wait a minute, please..." Claire came to the door and called down the corridor.

But Jan merely waved back at her and stumped off downstairs to Sister Thomas's sitting room.

Sister Thomas was no help.

"I'm sorry, Jan, but everyone has a placement he'd rather not do sometime or other and, you know, I'm always surprised how often he ends up enjoying it. You see, it's part of the European training regulations: you have to experience the work of every department before making your final choice of specialism. And, after all, it's only for a few weeks..."

It was like arguing with cotton-wool, thought Jan. Though there had been no argument, really, because he had no valid objections. None, at least, that he was prepared to share with Sister Thomas.

"You have no personal reasons for not wanting to work in the Mental Health Unit, do you?" Sister Thomas asked. Jan's face set hard and he shook his head. "I mean, no close friends who are currently being treated there or anything like that?" she went on. And she'd smiled at him so warmly, looked at him so closely, that Jan found himself blushing and backing out of the elegant little room, feeling more than a little foolish.

He strode along St Ag's drive, battling with the wind and his bad temper. He had to admit there was no reason for him to object to the placement except his own vague unease, and he wasn't going to admit that to anyone. He kicked up a mound of leaves and watched them scatter in the wind. Like all my plans, he thought bitterly.

Jan had many reservations about the training at St Ag's, not least because he had never intended to become a nurse. When he was air-lifted out of the battered hospital back home, he was working as a medic, as were many students who did not choose to join in the fighting. So when he arrived in England, the refugee authorities arranged for him to train at St Ag's. By the time Jan understood what was happening, it was too late to go back. And anyway, back to what? To where? Without his place at the hospital he'd doubtless be hanging round the huts on the ex-airfield which had become home to so many of his countrymen and women. At least he was comfortably housed, fed and, more important, kept usefully busy at St Ag's.

Until now, anyway. Jan stood in the hospital grounds in the wind and the rain, glaring at the bright lights of the huge building ahead. All those patients, all that medical work, all those drugs and lab tests, X-rays and CAT scans, all that exciting, scientific research, all that knowledge – and he had to end up in Mental Health!

He turned and peered through the driving rain across the grounds to the Mental Health department. No bright lights there, merely the spherical lamps outlining the patio which surrounded the low, stone-faced building. From where Jan stood it looked more like an outsize Japanese pagoda than a hospital department. Willows wept in the cobbled courtyard, water bubbled through coloured pebbles, and, from the hole in the centre of a huge millstone, a fountain burst, swivelled off-course just then by the wind. "Beautiful" and "peaceful", Nikki Browne had called it. Which it was, but it didn't look the least bit like a hospital to Jan. More like a holiday lodge up in the mountains back home, he thought. And what sort of medical treatments could be done in a hotel?

As he stared gloomily through the darkness, he saw someone slide a glass door back and step out on to the patio, standing, as he was doing, alone in the darkness and the pouring rain. He was wearing a tracksuit – Jan could just glimpse the white flashings on the jacket and trainers. Now, was he staff or was he a patient? wondered Jan.

But there was no way of telling.

Chapter 3

He was no happier about his placement next day. It was a soft, bright morning, almost summery, and even Jan had to admire the russet brick building glowing in the sunshine, surrounded by trees shedding red, brown and yellow leaves like coloured flakes. Compared with the hotchpotch of architectural styles that made up the main hospital – the Gothic splendour and inconvenience of the old Nightingale wing, the glassy tower of the main hospital block, and the scattered "temporary" buildings between – the Mental Health building was a little palace.

A Japanese palace, Jan reflected, as he searched for the main entrance. The glass sides of the octagonal building came down to ground level, but were heavily curtained and had no apparent door handles. He prowled along the terrace, feeling more and more uneasy as he peered into what could, after all, be people's bedrooms. What if someone drew back the curtains just as he was peering in? Jan winced at the thought and moved swiftly round a corner.

And here he found a small sign with "Entrance" beautifully painted in gold on a black wooden board with a long golden arrow pointing the way. Feeling rather like the poor son in a fairy tale, questing his way into the princess's castle, Jan followed the direction of the arrow.

And, lo and behold, a door! It was exactly like the rest of the glass panels except that it did have a handle – a gift from a fairy godmother. Jan smiled at his fanciful thought and tried the handle, pushing, pulling, and pushing again. Well, he'd failed the test; he was obviously not going to get the princess! Giving up the fairy-tale approach, he rattled the handle irritably, to no effect.

"Press and slide," said a light, husky voice behind him.

Jan turned and looked out over the terrace but saw no one. Was he hearing voices now? For a moment he was tempted to cross his fingers, superstitiously, as his grandmother had taught him.

"Press the hand-grip and then slide the door back," the voice said slowly in a flat northern accent. Nothing ethereal about that, Jan decided.

He looked down and saw the girl below him, sitting on one of the steps that led up to the entrance. Crumpled tracksuit, muddy trainers, off-white flashings, short, sweat-streaked blonde hair. Obviously not a fairy-tale princess, but what was she? Staff or patient? Jan couldn't make up his mind and dared not ask.

"Come on, I'll do it." She got up, gently pushed him aside and slid the door smoothly back, gesturing for him to enter.

"Student Nurse Jan Buczowski," she said, peering up to read the name badge on his pocket as he passed. "Well, Jan, once you've tackled that door everything's easy," she told him.

She certainly had an air of authority, Jan reflected, in spite of the informal dress. Maybe she was a member of the nursing staff; probably been out for her morning run before going on duty. Smiling, he turned to introduce himself, but she'd disappeared. Only a door swinging softly to the left of the hall showed where she'd gone. Like the Good Fairy in a children's story, thought Jan.

He looked around; this was obviously the reception area, except there was no one to receive him. Humming nervously to himself, he moved across to a noticeboard and began to read. Even there he couldn't make out the distinction between staff information and that aimed at patients. Courses on stress management, yoga, hypnotherapy and drug abuse overlapped with information about helplines, outings and discos. So who was this information for? Jan wondered.

As if in answer, the door crashed open and half a dozen tracksuited people scrambled in and stood panting by the entrance, not speaking. One by one, as they recovered their breath, they filtered off left and right through the swing doors. Except for one short, heavy man, whose sweat-stained tracksuit top showed that either he was terribly unfit or he was terribly fit and had just been on a very long run.

"Hey up, lad! What are you wanting?" he asked in a husky voice with a broad local accent.

"Ah – I – er – I – Jan Buczowski." Jan touched his badge, said his name and bowed slightly. Well, at last someone seemed prepared to receive him. He smiled expectantly.

But apparently the man was not expecting him. "You what?" he asked.

Jan took a deep breath. "I am Student Nurse Jan Buczowski," he said. "I am sent on placement to this department."

"Well, blow me down!" Without embarrassment, the short man stripped off his sweaty sweatshirt, screwed it up and rubbed vaguely under his arms with it. "Fancy you being our student!" he said.

"I beg your pardon?" asked Jan coldly.

The man walked over to the desk, his ancient trainers flip-flapping on the floor as he walked. He sat down behind the desk, opened a drawer, and took out a clipboard with several papers fastened to it.

"Aye, here it is – Week Seven, Student Placement." He frowned down at the top page thoughtfully. "Oh, I see now..."

Jan's heart leapt. There was some mistake; he was not expected. He could go back to Sister Thomas and tell her there was no placement in Mental Health...

"Ah well, Jan," said the man. He pronounced the name with a hard J, English-fashion. "You see, I thought you were Janet, or Janice, or Jane, I suppose. Any road up, I thought you were a lass." He looked up at Jan, eyes spilling over with humour. "It's your name, sithee – Jan..." He laughed.

"Please – my name?" Jan was puzzled and disappointed. Obviously if they'd got his name they were expecting him. The placement was on. But why did this man think his name was so funny? "It is not funny," said Jan firmly.

"No – you're right, lad, it's not funny in itself. It's just that I was expecting one of the little lasses from the nurse's home, like." He chuckled again, then stood up, holding out a well-worn hand. "Geoff Huckthwaite. Pleased to meet you, er, Jan."

Automatically, Jan took the proffered hand, wincing as the strong grasp enveloped his own. "Jan

Buczowski. Please to meet you." Though he felt far from pleased now he knew his placement was fixed.

"Right then, *Yan*." This time Charge Nurse Huckthwaite got it right. "Come and sit you down while I make meself decent."

So Jan found himself sitting in a small lounge with instructions to make two mugs of coffee – "two sugars in the panda mug" – in the little kitchen beyond, while Charge Nurse Huckthwaite – how on earth was he going to spell that in his reports? Jan wondered – went off to shower and change.

He didn't change much; Jan was surprised when he appeared once more in fresh sweatshirt and jeans. No white tunic, no blue tabs, no indication whatsoever that he was a Senior Charge Nurse, except for the usual name-badge worn by all staff, whatever their rank.

"Thanks, Jan." Geoff – he told Jan to call him that – picked up the mug with pandas on it. "I'm glad to see you can make yourself at home."

"Make yourself at home" was a phrase Jan had heard often since coming to England. At first it puzzled him, later it irritated him greatly. After all, he'd explained to Claire only that weekend, if you were at home you had no need to make yourself at home, and if you weren't, you couldn't. She had smiled at him and apologized for her over-hospitable relatives, making him feel more than usually guilty.

He winced at the memory and hastily glanced round at the room: television in the corner, shelves stacked with paperbacks and magazines, half a dozen low chairs and a couple of coffee tables. Plants on the window-sill, brass urn filled with dried grasses in the fireplace.

"It is like a home," he said.

But Geoff didn't looked pleased. "Not *a* home," he said. "More a home from home, if you see what I mean."

Jan didn't. "Is your coffee all right?" he asked, to cover his ignorance.

"Champion!" Geoff took a long draught from the panda mug and nodded.

Jan reached into his pocket for the notebook. "Champ-i-on," he muttered. "How do you spell?"

Geoff looked puzzled for a moment, then amused. "Ah, I see. Learning English as well as nursing, are you?"

Jan nodded. "All times when I hear new word, I write it down," he said.

"Every time," Geoff corrected.

Jan nodded. "Every time," he repeated.

Geoff gave a roar of laughter. "You'll have a rare old collection by the time you're done here," he said.

"Why is that?"

Geoff shrugged his huge shoulders. "Well, we're very informal here, as you might have noticed."

Jan nodded sternly.

"And sometimes, with our sort of patient, things get on top of them and they have to let fly. Are you with me?"

Another nod. Another frown.

Geoff cocked an amused eye at Jan's serious face. "So the language, d'you see, gets a bit ripe." He laughed softly.

"Ripe..." Jan repeated slowly. He was thinking hard. "Strong language, mayhaps?"

"Aye, just a bit." Geoff shook his head, though he still smiled broadly. "Only to be expected," he said. "After all, it's home from home here."

"What is this 'home from a home'?" Jan felt confident enough to ask now.

"Like being at home. Like you in the Nurses' Home. Which one are you in?"

"Kelham House."

"Aye. Well, that's what I mean. You have a little room, a little home of your own, away from all the hassles and cares of your studies, don't you?"

Jan nodded. "I am lucky," he said. People were always telling him that, and as far as accommodation was concerned, he had to agree with them.

"Yes, well, so are my folk here." Charge Nurse Huckthwaite plonked his mug on the table. "I'll show you around; you'll see what I mean."

The rest of the morning was a blur of names, smiles,

blank looks, surly glares and occasional handshakes. And what with Geoff's strong accent and his habit of referring to everyone by their first name, and the fact that the only white coat in the whole building seemed to be his own, Jan still couldn't work out who were staff and who were patients.

It was so much more difficult than being in a traditional ward. There, the first thing he did was to make a mental map of the beds and the names of the patients in them. Here, there was no chance of that; there wasn't a ward in sight – nor even a single bed.

Until Charge Nurse Huckthwaite found an unoccupied bedroom to show him. It was neatly furnished, in a style similar to Jan's room back at Kelham's. As they stood looking in at the door, Geoff explained that Jan must never enter anyone's room without knocking.

"We don't have locks, you see, for security reasons." He looked hard at Jan, to see whether he understood. "In case anyone's in danger and we need to get in."

"Ah," said Jan, eagerly. "In case of fire."

"Well, among other things." Geoff hesitated, then obviously decided against going any further with that subject. "Any road up," he went on, "to give people their privacy, we have a rule about not entering their rooms without being invited. Right?"

"Right." Jan made a mental note of Rule Number One: do not enter patients' rooms without knocking. He looked around the corridors. "But where are all the patients?" he asked.

"Good point." Geoff grinned. "Some of them will have gone across to clinics, others will be in occupational therapy, and some will be back in bed unless I go and rouse them. Come on!"

So Jan spent the next few minutes knocking loudly on doors while Geoff popped his head round the doors with a cheery greeting and a reminder of some appointment or other. Eventually they reached the last door before reception.

"Karen? Karen, come on now; you know Dr Hammond's clinic's at ten. Get your glad rags on and trot on over. Shall I send our new student in to help you?" He winked broadly at Jan. "Jan here –" he went back to saying the "J" as in Janet – "Jan'll be glad to give you a hand..."

"I'll bet he will!" The door opened quickly and Jan saw the small blonde girl who'd let him in. She was wrapped in a white towelling robe and rubbing her wet hair.

"Hi, Jan!" she said. "What's a nice boy like you doing with a dirty old man like Geoff?"

Jan blushed but Geoff merely laughed. "How did you know Jan was a lad?" he asked her.

"We've met," she said. "Don't think you know everything that goes on here, Geoff Huckthwaite." She threw Jan a bright smile. "I'll go straight over," she said, and closed the door.

"Met our Karen then, have you?" Geoff asked as they made their way across reception to the office.

Still blushing, Jan nodded. "She let me in this morning," he said. "Before you came back from your run."

"The little madam took a short cut and was back before us." But Geoff smiled almost fondly at the thought. "A month ago she couldn't get out of bed of a morning; now she's out running three times a week."

"Why?" Jan repeated.

"Why?" Geoff repeated incredulously. "Hast never heard of a healthy mind in a healthy body, lad?"

That phrase again! Jan nodded. "But this department is for the mind only, isn't it?"

Geoff nodded. "Aye, well, Clinical Depression is very debilitating, you know; low energy levels, disturbed sleep patterns – some people can't sleep at night so they tend to doze on and off all day. And when they first arrive we let 'em, but later we try to get them moving, just a bit at first; in the gym, out for walks, swimming – whatever they can face. It's the only bit of control they have over their lives, some of them."

"And this makes them well again?" Jan couldn't keep the scorn out of his voice. If the only thing these patients needed was a bit of exercise, what kind of nursing was he going to learn? Gymnastics and jogging?

Geoff looked up at him shrewdly. "Of course, they need a lot more besides," he said. "Therapy, counselling, yoga, relaxation – pills even. Depends on the patient, and which psychiatrist takes the case."

They were back in the office now, and as soon as Geoff sat down, the phone started ringing.

"Tell you what, Jan." He put his hand over the mouthpiece. "Just go and make sure Karen gets to Dr Hammond's clinic, will you? She's a dab hand at going missing."

Grimly, Jan strode back to Karen's room. So, his first assignment was escort duty! he thought. More like being a policeman than a nurse!

He knocked on the door and waited to be invited in. But when Karen appeared, she was dressed – black sweater, black leggings, biker boots, leather jacket – and apparently ready to go out.

"I might have known he'd send you back to check up on me." She glared up at him.

"No, I am here to escort you," said Jan, bowing slightly and smiling down at her, conscious of trying hard to charm the girl – something that gave him no trouble at all, usually.

But Karen didn't smile back; she just shrugged. "Please yourself," she said. "But I'm not going to Hammond's Horrors until I've had my coffee. Right?"

"Right," Jan agreed. "I will make you one right now."

"No, hang about – I go to the caff; they'll do me some toast. Hammond's bound to ask what I've eaten. Come on!" And slamming the door, she led him back to reception. This time, he slid the outer door open easily and stood back to let her through.

"Quick learner, aren't you?" she said coldly. But she allowed him to catch up with her and together they walked quickly across the dewy-damp grass towards the main building.

Once there, Karen suddenly changed; she stood stiffly in a corner at the top of the steps and refused to go through the door.

"I can't go in," she whispered.

"But you said you wanted to come over to the café," said Jan. "And if we don't hurry, the toast will be off." He put out a hand to her and for a moment she stood, staring at it as if she'd never seen a hand before.

"What's that for?" she demanded.

"To help you through the door," Jan said. "Remember how you helped me this morning? 'Once you've cackled the door,' you said, 'everything's easy'..."

Karen looked up at him through narrowed eyes. Then breathing hard, as if back from a run, she pulled herself upright.

"*Tackled*," she muttered.

"What?"

"The word's tackled, not cackled." She looked at him severely, like a very strict teacher.

But Jan's mistake seemed to have revived her; she took his hand and allowed him to lead her through the swing doors. He could feel her trembling right from her fingertips, just like some of the casualties back home – uninjured but shocked. So Jan did as he would have done there: he grasped Karen's upper arm, pulled her close and began speaking gently and softly into her ear as he guided her across the crowded entrance.

"Nearly there now, Karen. Just a bit further – steady – past the news shop – turn right here – soon be eating your tea and toast. Look, it's just over there!"

He looked up as he said that, just in time to see Claire Donovan coming out of the café, waving, smiling, moving quickly towards him. Suddenly conscious that he was holding Karen very close, he let go of her arm. Immediately she was off across the hall.

Avoiding Claire's welcoming smile, he pushed through the crowd. "Karen!" he called. "Karen, come back!"

He scanned the entrance eagerly, but saw only the puzzled hurt in Claire Donovan's eyes.

Chapter 4

With a muttered apology, Jan rushed on into the café. But a quick scan of the queue showed him that Karen had given up the idea of toast and coffee. He turned to leave and saw Claire standing just where he'd pushed past her. Jan groaned; he'd have to pass her again, and he could hardly ignore her this time.

"Claire! Sorry, I have no time – I'm with a patient. Did you see her? A small blonde girl in black – leather jacket, boots?"

"Yes, I did see her," Claire said. "With you," she added pointedly.

"I'm bringing her to the clinic," Jan explained. "But she's gone a runner." He looked wildly all round once more.

"*Done* a runner," Claire corrected. She looked at him closely. "You are all right, aren't you, Jan?"

He shook her off. "Of course I'm not all right. What if I've lost a patient?"

"Calm down, Jan." Claire put a hand on his arm. "She's probably only slipped off for a quick smoke."

Jan shook off the hand. "Did you see her go?" he asked impatiently.

"Yes, she went that way." Claire pointed down the main corridor. "See you this evening?" she called as Jan rushed off. Well, at least he didn't have to reply, he thought.

The corridor was wide, high and dim – part of the Nightingale building – and at that time of day it was seething with people. Jan nipped in and out, edging this person aside, dodging a wheelchair, overtaking a trolley, passing porters, patients and probably distinguished consultants for all he knew.

All he did know was that he couldn't see Karen. Inwardly cursing – in his own language – he lifted up his head to peer above the crowd but he knew it was hopeless; she was so small she would be quite hidden among all those people. At the junction that marked the start of the modern extension, he paused and mopped his face. Sweating! His hand was shaking too, and he suddenly felt quite dizzy. Damn! This was not the time, not the place… He stepped back into a quiet side corridor, leaned against the wall and rubbed his damp hands down his tunic.

He was suddenly reminded of Geoff Huckthwaite's stained tracksuit top. And of his words: "She's a dab hand at going missing." Well, whatever a "dab hand" meant, Karen certainly was one; she'd got away from him easily enough. Jan took a deep, shaky breath and tried to gather his thoughts into some coherent plan.

Suddenly he knew what to do; he'd go to Dr Hammond's clinic and report her missing. Yes, that was it; let someone else take the responsibility. He was here to train as a nurse, not a nursemaid. He stepped out into the concourse again and looked round for some signs. Now, where did Dr Hammond have his clinic?

Damn! He should have checked with Geoff before setting off. Or even with Karen, though he doubted whether she'd have told him the truth. In spite of his irritation, he smiled. That girl reminded him of some of the young soldiers at home, so certain and full of themselves – bravado they called it – and then suddenly, for no obvious reason, crumbling, just as she had at the main entrance. It had always embarrassed Jan back home; soldiers – even sixteen-year-old soldiers – should be cold and hard, not shivering in corners or quietly weeping.

But Karen hadn't wept, he remembered. She'd just stopped, as if paralysed, unable to get through the door. Yet even now she was on the run, probably enjoying all the trouble she was causing him. Well, he wasn't going to give her that satisfaction. Mobilized by the thought, he pushed his way across to the reception desk. There were the usual long queues but Jan's white coat had a magical effect; people stepped back to let him through.

"Where is Dr Hammond's clinic?" he asked the duty clerk.

"Hammond? Psychiatric?" The clerk took his eyes off the computer screen for a moment then paused, examining Jan's tense face curiously. Jan was irritated. Surely the clerk didn't think that he had an appointment with Dr Hammond?

"I have a message," he lied. And he pointed to his name-badge.

"Oh, right. Best take the lift. It's the tenth floor, Tower Block; you'll see the signs up there."

"Thanks!" Jan's heart sank. Across the lobby he could see small knots of people waiting for the lifts. More delay, more time for Karen to get wherever she was going. Well, wherever she was, she wouldn't be waiting for a lift, he suddenly realized. Anyone who panicked like she did in the crowded entrance wouldn't be happy squashed into a small space with a crowd of people. Claustrophobia, they called it. Jan remembered making a note of the word only a few weeks ago. Remembered, too, being shut into small spaces with the stench of unwashed patients, lamp-oil, dust and crude disinfectant in the hospital back home. He'd put his notebook away quickly then, shutting out the word and the memories.

And he shut them out now as he made his way to the Tower Block stairs. He knew them well; last term he'd been in Cytology on the fifth floor, and he'd run up the stairs every morning. Just for the exercise, he'd told himself, and anyway, there were always queues for the lifts.

He ran up the concrete steps now, flight after flight, sweating again and breathless, but somehow healthily, not sickened and dizzy as he had been a few minutes earlier. Maybe Geoff Huckthwaite's recipe for a healthy mind and body had some truth in it after all, he thought. Maybe he should take up running, or work out in the gym this winter, instead of going for walks with Claire. Jan sighed; it would be difficult to persuade Claire that he was doing it for his health and not just to avoid her. Not *just*, he repeated, and his feet drummed out the words as he plodded upwards – not just, not just...

Suddenly, on the landing of the eighth floor, he stopped. He could hear the steady plock, plock of rubber boots on the steps further up and a slight clink of metal, like the sounds of zips and rings on a biker's boots. Jan slowed down and moved quietly from step to step, trying to breathe steadily without panting. It wouldn't do for Karen to think she was being followed by a heavy-breather!

He caught up with her between the ninth and tenth floor, but only because she was sitting on the bottom step of the final flight, legs sprawled in front of her, cigarette on, for all the world as if she was relaxing on the sofa at home.

"Thought it'd be you," she said, blowing smoke at him. "Took your time."

"Karen!" Jan leaned against the balustrade, panting. "Put that cigarette out. You must know there is rule..."

"Oh, there's always a rule," said Karen. She took a deep drag on the cigarette. "But we're not bothering anybody here, are we? Want one?" She offered a crumpled pack to Jan.

He shook his head. In his country, before their war, most people smoked quite heavily, himself included. Even during the dark, half-starved, wartime days, people somehow managed to smoke something. Cigarettes became currency; you could even buy food with them. So it had been a shock to discover that many places in England did not allow smoking, like St Ag's. The whole of the hospital and the grounds were non-smoking areas – Kelham House too. And the cost of English cigarettes came as a shock too, so Jan had no alternative but to give up the habit which had sustained him through many appalling battles and raids. Now he barely remembered the taste and found it easy to refuse.

"Come on," he said. "Put that out and let's get up this last flight."

To his surprise she crushed out the stub on the floor – amongst several others, he noted with amusement. Even in a non-smoking hospital, the dedicated puffers – many of them medical staff – would find a little haven.

"Race you!" said Karen, setting off upstairs at a good pace.

But Jan's legs were longer, and his determination to keep her in sight was stronger. He leapt upstairs two at a time and almost pushed her through the door into the tenth floor.

Karen gripped his hand, as if he were the unwilling patient and she was in charge, and led him along a thickly carpeted corridor with doors at either side, like a hotel. Eventually it opened out to a lounge area, with a small desk at which sat an elegant older woman, working on the inevitable computer.

"Hi, Mrs Bradley!" Karen greeted her. "I've brought you a new one. Dr Hammond'll love him – he's a nutter!" And she laughed – a little too loudly, a little too much.

Jan blushed.

"Oh, don't mind Karen," Mrs Bradley reassured him, though she carefully checked his badge as she spoke. "Full of jokes and merry quips, aren't you, dear?"

As if she'd cleaned it off with a damp cloth,

Karen's smile disappeared. "Sometimes," she muttered. Letting go of Jan's hand, she flopped down in a corner – on the carpet, not a seat – and curled herself up, head down, knees up.

Ignoring Karen, Mrs Bradley nodded brightly at Jan. "Dr Hammond is running late," she said. "If you'd like to take a seat..." She leaned over the desk. "And keep an eye on her," she whispered.

So Jan sat beside the huddled figure of Karen, watching, waiting, thinking...

The last time he'd seen someone curled up like that had been a year ago. They'd been clearing the rubble from the hospital entrance so that ambulances could get through. Not a job for nursing staff, Jan would have been quick to point out at St Ag's, but back home you took on each and any job as you were needed. And it was almost a pleasant change from working inside the hospital, juggling drips and drugs and dressings and never having enough of any of them. Outdoors, in the crisp, clear air, with the light shimmering off the snowy mountains, Jan had relaxed, heaving great stones to one side, feeling, for once, fit and strong.

Until he shifted a pile of loose rubble with his shovel and saw the body, curled tightly, quite intact, no apparent injury, no blood, no broken bones – nothing to account for the screams of horror which seemed to come from nowhere, until he realized they came from himself...

Shaking himself free of the memory he saw Karen, sitting upright now, staring at him.

"You all right?" she asked in her husky voice.

Jan nodded – it was all he could do; his mouth was dry, his ears filled with pounding, his eyes staring into blackness, his hands shaking so much he couldn't even get them into his pockets to hide them.

"You don't look it," observed Karen. "Mrs Bradley, this new one's having an attack. Got any tranks?" Through the pounding and the mists, Jan was aware of her shrill laughter. Aware, too, of Mrs Bradley, bending over him, speaking low.

"Just sit still, Student Nurse Buczowski. Take a few deep breaths..." She moved out of his limited vision then and he felt his hand being gripped.

"Tell you what," Karen said, squeezing hard, "you can go in my place to see Dr Hammond. Honest, he's good."

In her place! The shock of it actually seemed to help for a moment. Did she really think he needed to see her psychiatrist – therapist – whatever he was? Jan breathed deeply and shook his head, though he soon gave that up when the world whirled round him.

"Karen?" A gentle voice called from the door. "Are you ready? Lovely to see you looking so smart..."

Jan saw a short man emerge from one of the rooms off the lounge. He felt Karen stiffen and now she was gripping his hands for her own comfort, not his.

"Right," she said flatly. "Just doing a bit of therapizing on my nurse." She turned to Jan. "Be all right, will you?" And, as he nodded, she stuck her head in the air and tramped over to the open door.

Mrs Bradley appeared, carrying a mug of coffee.

"Here you are, Student Nurse Buczowski. Sit back and sip this – it's very sweet."

It was! Jan took a wobbly, tentative sip and winced. He was often disparaging of the sweet, milky concoction which passed for coffee in England, but he found himself reluctantly relishing this stuff.

"There! You're looking better already," said the observant Mrs Bradley. "Gave you a shock, did she, our Karen?" She looked at him curiously. "You did well getting her here – I'd given her up. She's a naughty girl, that one." But she smiled almost affectionately at the thought. "And I expect you started off this morning without breakfast, late, rushing around?"

Jan nodded, too exhausted to correct her errors. And anyway, they might not be errors. OK, so he'd had a good breakfast, but maybe that was the trouble – rushing up ten flights of stairs on top of a heavy meal? Yes, that surely was what had knocked him out. He took a gulp of coffee.

Mrs Bradley nodded. "You youngsters don't realize what a strain nursing is. You must keep yourself fit if you're to help other people get better." She moved back to her desk. "Now, I'll ring Geoff Huckthwaite and tell him you're going off..."

"No!" Jan leapt to his feet, recklessly spilling coffee. "No, I shall take Karen back home..."

"Home?" Mrs Bradley looked startled.

"Back to the home," he corrected himself. "I'll talk with Geoff then, please?" He turned his most charming smile on to her, not realizing how dark were his eyes and the patches beneath, how ghastly white his face. "See, I'll drink up my coffee and feel fine." He sat down and drained the remainder of the coffee.

"Well, if you're sure..." Mrs Bradley's hand hovered over the telephone.

"I am sure," said Jan. And, as if to prove it, he picked up a magazine from the table and made a pretence of reading. "I will wait," he said, frowning at the words which danced up and down on the page in front of his eyes, but seeing only the body huddled under the pile of rubble.

Chapter 5

He didn't talk with Geoff, though – not about feeling ill. On the way back to Mental Health Karen had been very subdued, disappearing to her room as soon as they arrived, without even a wave or a word of thanks. Geoff had been busy in the office so Nurse Hawley had introduced herself and taken Jan off to the pharmacy to show him the drug regimes they used.

That was more like real nursing! Jan forgot all about his morning's troubles, impressed Nurse Hawley by producing his ever-ready notebook, and spent the rest of the morning helping her to check the stock in the drug cupboards. It was the kind of meticulous, well-defined task he found so satisfying. By lunchtime he was quite recovered – there was no need to mention anything to Geoff Huckthwaite.

"Everything all right with Karen?" he'd asked Jan over lunch in the cafeteria.

"Gave me the slip in here," Jan admitted. He decided he'd better be honest about that. "But I caught up with her – smoking on the stairs." He grinned, as if the nightmare chase had been merely a game. "Mrs Bradley says she's a naughty girl."

Geoff snorted. "Eeh, that Dr Hammond! He thinks they're all just naughty girls and boys. Give 'em plenty to do and a bit of dope to keep them happy, that's his remedy."

"Does it work?" Jan asked.

Geoff Huckthwaite shook his head. "Nothing works," he said. "Not on its own."

"But you have all those drugs…" Jan had been amazed at the number and variety of pills he'd seen that morning. In Cytology he'd soon become accustomed to learning complex drug regimes but he'd thought Mental Health would be all chat and therapy, not pills.

"Oh, drugs…" Geoff pronged a huge piece of sausage on to his fork and looked at it gloomily. "They have their place, of course, but they're no substitute for a bit of TLC and discipline." He chewed thoughtfully. "And even then we're often too late."

"This TLC, it is electric?" Jan asked. He'd heard of such treatments back in his own country before the war. One of his aunts had been ill after her daughter died, and there had been talk of some electrical treatment to make her better again. "But how can a few electrical impulses make up for the loss of a child?" Jan's mother had asked. And his father had smiled sadly and shaken his head.

As Geoff Huckthwaite was doing right now. "Tender Loving Care," he was saying.

"Pardon?" Jan automatically felt in his pocket for his notebook.

"Nay, put that away," said Geoff. "This isn't a bit of your medical jargon. TLC – tender loving care – the most important method of treating any ailment from eczema to schizophrenia. Pills alone can't cure and, frankly, neither can hospital. There's no prescription for peace of mind, tha knows."

And all through the afternoon, as Jan checked records, typed notices for the board, made tea for everyone, chatted to patients in the lounge, listened to Geoff running through their current work-load and helped Nurse Hawley walk a panic-stricken agoraphobic around the terrace, those words lived on in his mind.

Peace of mind – peace of anything – was something he'd had very little of in the past two years, he thought. But was he going to find peace amongst the troubled Mental Health patients in St Ag's?

At five o'clock he went to the office to check out with Geoff. The door was open and he could see

Geoff, sitting pushed back from the desk, looking up at the ceiling, arms loose by his sides, head lolling slightly. Asleep? Jan wondered, somewhat shocked by the idea. What should he do – wake Geoff up or just go quietly off duty without checking? As Jan stood at the door, pondering this dilemma, Geoff suddenly yawned loudly, stretched broadly and shook himself awake.

"Knackered," he said without apology.

And Jan, remembering Geoff's return from the early morning run, nodded in agreement.

"I suppose you're the same," Geoff went on. "It's harder for you."

"But I started later," said Jan.

"Today you did; tomorrow you can join us on the run. Right?"

Jan nodded. Well, it would fit in with his resolution to get fit. "You start from here?" he asked.

"Yes, eight o'clock. Tracksuit and trainers – and something comfortable for the rest of the day; you don't need that tunic here," Geoff said.

Jan thought of the thick, dark blue tracksuit issued by the refugee committee on his arrival in England. No two-tone jacket, no snazzy flashings – just fluffy-lined navy-blue cotton jersey. He'd slept in it on many a bitter cold night in his hut back at the base in Norfolk last winter. But he'd never appeared in public wearing it – yet.

"Right, I'll be here at eight," he told Geoff.

Geoff stood up. "Off you go, then. Write up your notes – and your new words." He grinned at Jan. "Knackered's a useful one."

Jan smiled. "Oh, yes," he said. "I have that already."

"Went all right, then, did it?" Nick Bone asked.

Jan hesitated, then nodded. "All right," he said doubtfully.

"But...?" Nick urged.

"But it is not like medical work," said Jan. "It is like ... caretaking."

"Caretaking?" Nick looked puzzled. "You mean you were emptying the bins, cleaning the building?"

"No, I mean I was taking care of the patients – just watching them."

"Oh!" Nick laughed as he understood him. "Well, I dare say there's a lot of that to do. I suppose they need company as much as anything."

"You mean just sitting with them – that is part of the treatment?"

"I dunno, but it can't do much harm, can it?"

Jan's face suddenly brightened. "TLC!" he said.

"What?"

"It is what Geoff – the Charge Nurse – told me. Tender loving care, he said..."

But Nick wasn't interested in Geoff's medical theories.

"Geoff – is that what you call your Charge Nurse?" he asked.

"He told me to."

Nick frowned. "Never heard of a student on first-name terms with a Charge Nurse; not on the ward, anyway."

"But there is no ward – that's another thing. It is like – well, like living here, I suppose." Jan gestured round Kelham's elegant entrance hall. "The patients have their own rooms, a bit like ours, a kitchen, a lounge like our common room; most of them have their own things with them too: radio, small television set, you know..."

"I know," Nick agreed ironically. "More gear than us nurses."

Not more than he had though, reflected Jan. Nick's room was crammed with all the latest technology – TV, CD, computer, CD-ROM – all bought cheap on trips abroad, he'd told the others.

"But you see, it's a 'home from a home', Geoff says," he explained to Nick.

"Well, I can see why you're not keen on things there – more like an old folks' home. Why don't you take your fiddle and give them a sing-song?"

"No, tomorrow I must go in my tracksuit and take them for a run." Jan sighed, thinking once more of that awful garment.

"Wow! Funny sort of nursing, that is. Can you do it?"

"Oh, I can do it," said Jan. "I was thinking of doing some running to get fit this winter, so I don't mind that."

"But...?"

Jan shrugged. "It's just that I have only a baggy old tracksuit, very heavy and thick. And there is not time to find a new one." Nor money, he added to himself.

Nick was looking him up and down thoughtfully. "You can take one of mine," he said.

"Oh, I couldn't do that!"

"Why not? I'm in college all day tomorrow – I shan't be doing any running. And in any case, the one I'm offering is too long in the legs for me. Come on!"

They went upstairs to Nick's room. When he opened the wardrobe, Jan couldn't stop a sharp gasp.

"A bit over the top, eh?" said Nick, surveying the dozens of suits, jackets, shirts, sweaters, trousers, ties, the many pairs of shoes. "I've let my own place off so I had to clear everything out," he said apologetically. "Now, where's that green shell-suit?"

Blue flashings it had, not white, but it was nevertheless a beautiful suit – and it fitted Jan perfectly.

"There you are, Student Nurse Buczowski – your new uniform!"

"Ah, no – I'll bring it back tomorrow."

Nick shrugged. "Keep it, old son; I never use it. Too lazy to need a tracksuit – and I've got another if ever I should feel the urge to take exercise. Now, what about a drink down in the medics' bar?"

Jan looked at the shimmering green nylon slung over his arm. "I'm buying," he said.

Luckily, having been in Ireland with Claire's family for the last few days, Jan had spent very little that week, so he was able to get the first round in. But Nick insisted on buying the next, then a couple of friends of his joined them and someone else bought, and after that, Jan lost count.

And almost lost his footing as he stumbled up the stairs at Kelham's. Nick and his friends had gone on to watch a video, but Jan was conscious of having an early start next morning and of being very hungry, so he'd left. There might be the makings of a sandwich in the kitchen, he thought – mayhaps. He giggled at his deliberate mistake, stumbled over the top step and fell in a heap on the landing. He lay for a moment half stunned, then made as if to rise. But he couldn't; his head was spinning and he was sweating again. And he knew this was not caused by his fall but by the memory of other corridors, other stairs, of pushing crowds, splintering glass, bulging walls. He clung on to the carpet and felt it shift beneath him. Don't vomit, he told himself as the blackness descended.

* * *

"Jan! What are you doing? Are you hurt? Come on, let me help you up..." Claire's soft, sweet voice came from some distance above him. He felt her sit on the step next to him, gather his shoulders, turn him over. "Oh, Jan!" he heard her exclaim. "You've been drinking!" And he heard the disappointment in her voice.

Quickly sobered, he pushed her away and scrambled to his feet.

"I've been for a drink with Nick," he mumbled.

"So I see," said Claire coldly. "And more than one, I guess."

"A few," Jan admitted. But why should he feel guilty? This was the first night since his student days at home – over a year ago, now – that he'd had more than a couple of lagers, which was probably why they'd affected him so much, he excused himself. Suddenly overcome with weariness, he drooped unsteadily against the wall and yawned widely. "I must sleep," he announced, making to move past Claire.

"You must eat," said Claire firmly. "And I'll make some coffee. Come on."

She pushed him towards the kitchen, where he slumped into a chair and propped his heavy head in his hands. Without speaking, Claire made sandwiches and coffee and thrust them across at him.

"Thank you," said Jan with as much dignity as he

could muster. He chewed at a sandwich hungrily, took a sip of hot coffee and suddenly felt better. "Thanks," he said again, and he smiled, very slightly, at Claire, who sat opposite, clutching a mug of coffee but not drinking.

Suddenly aware of her silence, he picked up another sandwich. "This I need," he said.

"Need this." Claire spoke.

"What?"

"I need this – or I needed this; that's the way we say it."

"Ah, yes. I need this," Jan repeated, vaguely feeling for the notebook. Failing to locate it, he gave up and concentrated on eating. When he'd finished the last sandwich, he sat back, mug in hand.

"You had supper in the cafeteria?" he asked, suddenly conscious that he'd not offered her any of the sandwiches.

Claire shook her head. "I was waiting," she said.

"Waiting?"

"To have it with you."

Jan was horrified. "But we should have shared the sandwiches," he protested. "I thought you made them for me."

"I did," she said. "I had a snack earlier when I realized you'd gone out."

"Oh, good," he smiled, feeling it wasn't really good at all, though he couldn't quite think why.

"I waited," Claire said again, very clearly,

"because I thought we were going to eat together, either here or over in the café – or maybe down at Dukes."

Dukes was the local pub, "The Duke of Wellington", where many of the medics had their suppers whenever funds allowed. Jan's never did, though he'd often joined the Kelham Six for a drink there.

"Did we arrange this?" he asked, genuinely puzzled and a little alarmed. Surely his funny turns couldn't be affecting his memory?

Claire blushed. "Well, not exactly," she admitted. "I just assumed..."

Jan stared at her. "Is this what you do in England?" he asked. "Go everywhere together, do everything together, because we are –" he gestured vaguely, unable to find a word to describe their relationship – "together?"

"Of course not!" Claire said fiercely. "It's just that as we're not actually together all day, I thought you'd want – I mean – well, for us to meet in the evenings ... sometimes," she ended lamely.

"Sometimes, yes," Jan agreed. The food was beginning to affect him; all he wanted to do now was to roll into bed and sleep. "But this evening we had no arrangement."

"No, we hadn't," Claire agreed sadly. "Sorry."

Jan tried to work out whether she was sorry they hadn't arranged to meet or sorry she'd assumed they would eat together. But the effort was too much; he felt utterly exhausted and not a little guilty and he suddenly snapped.

"So what is this 'sorry'?" he asked. "It is I who must be sorry. I did not think enough…"

"Enough of me?" she asked, anxiously.

"No, I mean not enough thinking … what is it?" Jan scowled with the effort of fighting off exhaustion and finding the right word. "Thoughtless!" He brought it out triumphantly. "I was thoughtless; I am very sorry." He gave a great sigh and propped his head up again. "And very tired," he added. "And tomorrow I must run."

"Run?" Claire was startled.

"We have a morning run. Good therapy, Geoff says. And I must join; it is part of the treatment."

"For them or for you?" asked Claire.

Jan took her amused tone to mean he was forgiven. "For both, I hope," he said. "I think I need exercise too."

"I think you need therapy too," said Claire, looking straight at him.

He stood up suddenly, roughly pushing the chair away. "Why do you think this?" he demanded. "You think I am a nutter just because I don't take you to supper?" He felt himself shaking – with anger, he hoped it was nothing else.

"No, no," soothed Claire. "I just mean you are having symptoms of stress; admit it. Good heavens!

It would be very strange if you didn't, after all you've been through."

"No!" Jan was shouting now, gripping the back of his chair so hard that his knuckles stood out white and bony, and he felt the blood drain from his face. "I have no symptoms, no stress. You think because I have a few drinks I am alco … alho … alcholic." The word eluded him.

"I didn't say that." Claire glared at him. "I mean, just look at you – you're stressed out right now!"

There was a moment's pause. They faced each other over the table, dark eyes blazing into grey, both faces white with anger, overlaying other emotions – concern in Claire, fear in Jan.

Suddenly he spoke. "Stressed? *Maybe*." He got the word right for once. "But who is stressing me?" he asked.

He turned abruptly and left the room.

Chapter 6

It was just his luck, it seemed to Jan, that the weather changed overnight. A westerly wind had sprung up, ripping the last of the leaves off the trees and scattering them wildly up into the lowering sky. Rain was already spitting down as he ran across the lawns to the Mental Health building.

At least he knew the way to get in today. He slid the door open and, closing it, leaned on the glass, breathless already.

"You'd best dump your bag in the office," Geoff greeted him. "And lock it after you. Make haste – we're nearly ready!"

But when Jan came back he found only four prospective runners.

"Lazy lot!" said Geoff. He turned to a youngster

who was sitting gazing blankly at nothing. "Take a run round, Martin; bash at a few doors."

The boy got up, stiff as an old man, and plodded off down the corridor. Jan could hear him knocking and calling. He looked round at the other three members of the party – all men – all ignoring him and each other, standing, leaning, one running gently on the spot, murmuring something to himself. Jan pulled on the zip of Nick's tracksuit and reflected that he needn't have bothered to borrow it; no one would have noticed his shabby blue one.

But suddenly the door burst open and Karen ran in.

"Good! Just in time," she said. "Hi, Geoff! Hi, Jan!"

She jumped up and down, did a few bends and came up looking wonderful, skin glowing, eyes shining, lips smiling.

"What have you been taking?" Geoff asked suspiciously.

Karen scowled. "Well, thank you, Nurse Huckthwaite," she said. "Here I am, full of positive thoughts and natural good humour, all ready to race the lot of you round the track, and all you can do is accuse me of being high!" She put out her tongue at Geoff and blew a very noisy raspberry.

Jan couldn't help smiling, though he looked anxiously across at Geoff, who grinned and slapped Karen on the shoulders.

"OK, I'm sorry. It's just that we haven't seen you like this for a week or two." He glanced at Martin, who had just returned from his recruiting trip and was about to collapse on the sofa again. "No more takers, Martin?" he asked. "Right, let's be off then!"

They started slowly, jogging rather than running, in pairs. To his disappointment, Jan found himself bringing up the rear with Martin; Karen had taken the lead with Geoff. Well, at least that saved him having to make conversation, he thought. Martin was obviously on automatic pilot, and running right into the wind was hard going. Jan had assumed he was pretty fit after the hard living of the past year. Certainly he hadn't an extra ounce of weight, he'd stopped smoking, rarely drank (except for last night, he reminded himself, grimly) and, although he'd done no organized exercise, he was always on the move in and out of the hospital, up and down steps and stairs...

But he'd forgotten how he'd sat over his books and notes and in lectures every day and many nights last half-term. And the Irish hospitality over the holiday; he'd been feeling heavier since he got back from Claire's family. Another pang of guilt hit him when he thought of their kindness and her obvious concern for him.

No time to brood, however; the track led uphill through the woods and the going was hard. Leaf-mould and mud clung to his trainers and he was tempted to drop out for a moment to clean them off. But Martin pounded on grimly, as if driven by clockwork, and the others were out of sight.

Geoff had pushed him to the back, with the muttered instruction that Jan should pick up any stragglers. Remembering how easily Karen had escaped him, Jan put on a spurt and pulled alongside Martin. The track had levelled out now, the pace was easy. The rain fell steadily, dripping off the trees into his hair and down his neck. His feet were sodden, the beautiful tracksuit mud-splattered, but Jan felt quite light-hearted. Like Karen had looked before they'd started out, he reflected; a sudden surge of well-being and energy, all stress fallen away. Unconsciously he quickened his pace.

"Come on, Martin," he called. "Let's catch up with the others."

He glanced back and saw the boy following, hair plastered flat against his skull, eyes dead, rain streaming down his face. Or was it rain? Something in the boy's expression made Jan pause. He looked like those young soldiers, down from the mountains, snow-soaked and dazed...

"You all right?" he asked as Martin came up.

The boy merely gasped for breath – or was he sobbing? Jan didn't wait to check. After all, what could he do if Martin was weeping? He edged away from the answer to that.

"How much further?" he asked.

Martin shook his head hopelessly. He didn't care, Jan realized. So shut up in his own despair, it didn't matter to him whether he was out there getting soaking wet or in his room warm and dry – and still depressed.

I know the feeling, Jan thought. And, shocked by his admission, he stumbled over a tree root and fell. Retreating to his own language, he cursed loudly and scrambled up. Martin never even turned to see what he'd done.

"You've made a right muck-up of your tracksuit," observed Karen when Jan ran in last. "And we beat you!" She was sitting on the terrace, taking off her shoes.

"You did not," said Jan. "I was to be last in case anyone..." He realized how tactless that was going to sound.

"...got away," Karen finished. "Not today, mate," she grinned. "Shoes off, young Martin! You too," she told Jan.

Martin stood, one-legged, fumbling with his laces, rain and tears dripping off the end of his nose as he bent his head. Jan felt he should help in some way, but he couldn't help a grown boy to undo his shoelaces, could he? He stood watching, helplessly trying to figure out what to do.

Karen pushed between them. "Come on, lad, let's be having you. Here, sit down." She pushed him on to a bench, mopped Martin's wet face with her handkerchief and bent to unfasten his shoes. "Right! Hot shower for both of us, I reckon, eh, Martin?"

She put an arm around the boy's shaking shoulders and led him indoors. Jan sat on the bench and removed his shoes, feeling helpless, useless and wishing he was anywhere but in the Mental Health department of St Ag's. After all, he told himself angrily, even in the blasted-out wreck of Czerny Infirmary he'd been useful. Here, even the patients knew more than he did.

He pushed his way into the entrance, hoping to catch up with Karen, but she'd done her usual disappearing act. With Martin? Jan wondered.

"He's a bright lad," Geoff said at coffee break. "But not as bright as his parents think he is."

"And that is his trouble?" asked Jan.

Geoff shrugged. "Some of it," he said.

They were in Geoff's sitting room, sharing coffee and doughnuts. Showered, wearing his usual jeans and sweatshirt, Jan felt healthier than he had done for a long time. Running, he decided, was definitely going to be his new hobby. He'd get to know the patients better, get himself fit, and never have another of his funny "turns".

"Now then, what've we got for you today?" Geoff pulled his clipboard closer.

"Nurse Hawley asked me to put the new drugs list into the computer," said Jan happily.

"Did she?" Geoff looked hard at Jan. "Yes, well, you can do that this afternoon. This morning we've got group therapy."

Jan's expression registered his dismay. "Group therapy," he repeated.

"You don't have to take part – just sit in on it," Geoff beamed. "You'll need to get some idea of all the different treatments we use – for your file, at least."

"Ah, yes," Jan nodded. "And the running, is that for my file also?"

Geoff grinned. "Please yourself," he said. "That's my bit of voluntary work."

"It did not seem to help Martin," Jan observed. "But Karen was full of – er –"

"Beans," supplied Geoff. "Yes, well, don't be foxed by Karen. When she's high she's very, very high. When she's low, she's rock bottom."

Jan remembered how Karen had collapsed at the clinic the previous day. "This I have seen at home," he told Geoff, surprising himself with the reference.

"Aye," Geoff nodded. "And a few like Martin, I'll be bound."

Jan looked away, out through the window. Grey, no sun, no light, not even a breath of wind now, just the drip, drip of drizzle and the blank grey fog.

"Depression," he said. "That is what he suffers?"

"He does that," Geoff agreed. "Clinical depression. I expect you'd see a lot of that back home?"

"No, not a lot," said Jan. "It was funny, when you think how we were trying to live in that city; no water, no electricity, no food, no medical supplies and the bombardment going on, on, on..." He took a shaky breath. This was the first time he'd spoken to anyone about his experiences back home and he wasn't quite sure why he was talking to Geoff. "But people were not depressed," he went on. "Not like Martin. They weep, they cry, they are hungry, cold, frightened – but not depressed. I wonder why this is?"

"Same in Northern Ireland," said Geoff. "All those years of bombs and shootings, but the cases of breakdown and suicide actually went down." He took a sip of coffee and looked at Jan shrewdly. "Won't be the same in peace-time, I'll bet you."

"What do you mean?"

"It's as if people put off having a breakdown. They're too busy struggling to survive – no time for mental health problems. Then, when peace breaks out as it were, it all comes tumbling down."

"'Tumbling down'," Jan repeated thoughtfully. "So, you think when there is peace in my country there will also be stress?"

Geoff nodded. "And a need for psychiatric nursing," he said pointedly. He stood up. "So we'd better get on with your training, else you won't be ready to go back."

Go back? Jan pondered this idea as he followed Geoff down the corridor to a seminar room. Back to what? No home, no parents that he knew of, no university to continue his studies. No, he would never go back there.

"Here we are!" Geoff opened the door and ushered Jan into the room ahead of him.

The first thing that struck him was the silence. It wasn't the kind of hush that falls when someone enters and conversation dies. Jan had the distinct feeling that there had been no conversation, even before he came in.

And no one looked towards the door. On half a dozen chairs, set well apart but in a perfect circle, sat four women, a middle-aged man, and the boy, Martin, who was slumped forward, examining the pattern on the carpet. One woman hugged herself close and rocked gently from side to side; an elderly woman with a halo of fine white hair sat rigidly upright, eyes tight shut, apparently fast asleep; the others stared at the wall in front of them.

"Good morning, everybody." Geoff spoke heartily. "Are we all here?"

No one replied.

"Now then, who've we got, today?" Geoff looked round the circle. "There's Alan –" he indicated the older man – "and Margaret." He nodded towards the rocker. "Susan, Anna and Frieda." The last was the older lady, who nodded graciously but never opened an eye. "And, of course, Martin you've met. This is Jan, our student nurse. You know him already, don't you, Martin?" Geoff said pointedly.

Martin lifted his eyes for a second, nodding vaguely, then looked alarmed as the door opened once more.

Jan turned to see Karen, in full leather gear.

"Hello, hello, hello!" she said busily. "More chairs, Geoff – unless you're going to stand inside the kissing circle?" She laughed too much at the joke. "Can I have first go?" she said.

"Nah then, Karen!" Geoff spoke quietly. "Calm yourself and come on in. Jan will get us some more chairs."

"Oh, thanks very much, Jan." Karen looked across at Jan and smiled sweetly. "Sure you can manage?"

"I can manage," Jan said, copying Geoff's gentle tone. It seemed to work: as soon as the chairs were set – with mathematical precision – into the circle, everyone, including Karen, settled back and looked expectantly at Geoff.

Jan felt in his pocket for his notebook, but Geoff frowned and motioned him to leave it where it was. Jan obeyed, though he was worried he would miss something if he had no notes.

In fact, by the time they finished, he felt he'd missed everything. No matter how carefully he listened, how hard he concentrated, he didn't hear anything that seemed at all important. Geoff started by inviting the patients to tell the group how they were feeling, how they were coping, what they'd been doing since the previous meeting and, in their various ways, they told him. Some hesitated, others twittered on at great length and little relevance. Martin merely nodded to any question Geoff put to him; Karen did a cabaret act, flirting outrageously with anyone who caught her eye, and suddenly gave up mid-sentence, slumping down in her chair and turning her back on the group.

Geoff didn't even react to this. He listened, prompted, asked the occasional question, but otherwise remained silent, watchful. He could have been interviewing them for a job, not treating them for an illness, Jan reflected. Geoff took no notes, carried no files, and, of course, did not wear a white coat. Jan wondered whether the patients had got more out of the session than he had.

After about an hour, Geoff sat back and stretched his arms above his head. "Anything more to say?" he asked. There was no response. "So everybody's happy, are they? Everything's hunky-dory, is it?"

There was a stultifying silence. Jan was just deciding what he was going to have for lunch when Margaret suddenly stopped rocking and pointed at him.

"What about that one?" she said accusingly. "He

hasn't had a go."

"Neither he has," agreed Geoff. "What shall we ask him?"

"Well, I mean, what's he *for*?" she said.

Jan's eyes widened in dismay as Geoff said softly, "Well, Jan, what do you think you're for?"

Everyone sat up expectantly. Even Karen turned round. Unable to think of an answer, Jan looked desperately round for help; surely Karen would come out with some witty comment or other? But she only stared at him sullenly.

"Jan?" Geoff prompted gently.

"I … er … I do not understand the question," Jan finally brought out.

Geoff turned to the others. "You see, Jan here, he's from a country that's at war with itself. His English is better than mine, but he can't always follow what we're on about."

There was silence then as eight pairs of eyes regarded him with curiosity. Suddenly Alan spoke.

"I think Margaret means what's he *here for*?" he said.

"Ah! Well, I am here to learn all about nursing," Jan said, relieved to have an impossible question reduced to a simple one.

"If your country's at war, I should have thought you could have learned a lot more about nursing at home than over here," Alan pointed out.

"I did learn – was learning – but there we have no

medicines, no drugs or dressings, no hospitals now…" Suddenly assailed by the memory of his final morning at Czerny Infirmary, Jan stopped. Alan was right, he thought. What on earth was he doing at St Ag's, sitting in a circle chatting to "nutters", when his own people were still under bombardment, his parents still missing? He closed his eyes for a moment and tried to shut out the memory.

When he opened them, Frieda was looking straight at him, her own eyes startlingly blue and clear, seeming to see right through him.

"But you'll be a better nurse when you go back qualified," she smiled.

Jan stared at her as if he didn't understand. "Go back" – there it was again, that assumption that he would return home to his country some day. But since the day he got out, Jan had never once considered going back, never given a conscious, waking thought to the past. Even Granya and his parents were kept tucked away as if they were only photographs in an album. Now he closed his eyes, shut out Frieda's clear gaze, took a shaky breath and stood up.

"Sorry, I must go. Sorry – Geoff?" He turned to ask permission, but couldn't speak.

Geoff looked shrewdly at him and nodded. "Best be off, lad," he said in his easy way. "Dinnertime anyway."

* * *

Jan sat alone in the office, breathing heavily, waiting for the panic to subside. Damn! He'd felt so well that morning, quite glad to be back in the MH centre and quite proud to have done the run – even at the back. He looked across to the radiator where he'd hung the tracksuit to dry. Suddenly he got up, pulled off his sweatshirt and jeans, scrambled into the still-damp suit, and quickly let himself out on to the terrace. There he changed his shoes and set off through the mist, along the running track, breathing steadily now, striding smoothly. Panic over.

Chapter 7

The following week Jan ran every day, sometimes with the patients, more often alone, pounding along the track without a thought in his head. It seemed to do the trick; as long as he stuck to the running and to work, he had no recurrence of the panic symptoms. That was the solution, then – work and run, run and work.

"Physician, heal thyself," he quoted triumphantly. And he was healing very well up to now.

But weekends were different: no work to go to, all his friends around – he knew he'd find it difficult to keep to his solitary routine.

On Saturday morning he returned to Kelham's from his run, taking the stairs two at a time and landing in the kitchen without even breathing heavily.

"Ah! The elusive Mr Buczowski!" Katie greeted him. "Just in time to help me open this."

She handed him a square cake tin. "I've already broken two nails trying to get the lid off that old tin," she said. "I'll never shift my dad into the Tupperware age."

Jan had no idea what Tupperware was, but he obligingly sat down and eased his strong fingers around the lid. Eventually it slid off, revealing a square of sticky brown cake. Jan sniffed the pungent, spicy aroma and felt quite sick.

"Gingerbread!" he said. "Like we make at Christmas..." He choked and pushed the cake tin away from him.

"It's parkin," Katie explained. "My mam used to make it for Bonfire Night. Dad's taken over now."

Jan stared at her. This was the first time he'd heard her mention her mother, who, he suddenly remembered, had died just before Katie had arrived at St Ag's. For a moment he was tempted to ask her how she'd felt at the time; perhaps she too had "funny turns"?

"Dad's a whizz at making parkin now," Katie went on hurriedly, as if reading his thoughts. "You're coming to the bonfire, aren't you?"

"What is this bon-fire?" he asked cautiously.

"'*Please to remember the fifth of November, with gunpowder, treason and plot*,'" Katie chanted. "You know – Guy Fawkes?"

Jan shook his head.

"Well, he and some other men tried to blow up Parliament." Katie sat on the edge of the table and settled to her subject. "But somebody told the King's men and Guy Fawkes's gang were rounded up, tortured and executed – you understand?"

Jan shuddered. He understood it; it was the kind of treason and plot that was going on right now in his country. "When did this happen?" he asked.

"Sixteen hundred and something."

"But why did they plot?"

Katie shrugged. "They were Roman Catholics and the King and parliament were Protestant – you know, Church of England?"

This time Jan nodded. After all, his country was – had been – Catholic.

"And you eat gingerbread to celebrate these Catholics?" he asked.

Katie laughed. "Well, I don't know how the gingerbread – the parkin – got in there. But we have a bonfire and burn the guy – a model, you understand – and let off fireworks and eat treacle toffee, baked potatoes, hot-dogs..."

"Hot-dogs are American," Jan protested.

"Yeah – well, I think they came in later." Katie slid off the table. "Anyway, there's going to be a bit of a 'do' tonight – rather belated, I know, but the weather was lousy last week. We're building the bonfire right outside the children's ward this afternoon. Why don't you come and help?"

Jan hesitated. The last thing he wanted to get involved with was bangs and burning; he'd seen quite enough of those. On the other hand, he realized he'd been avoiding the gang – and Claire – all week.

"I'll come to build the bong fire," he said, leaving the rest of the invitation unanswered.

Katie laughed at his pronunciation. "*Bonfire.* You know – something to do with bones, I think." She shuddered. "Guy Fawkes wasn't the only one to be burned on a fire."

Jan repeated the word automatically, blocking out the implication. "Bonfire," he said. "I'll go and write that down."

"And meet us all downstairs after lunch. Nick's borrowed a truck to round up all the wood and stuff, Nikki's making a wonderful guy, and I'm just off to buy the fireworks. I'll be after contributions later – a fiver a head, all right?" Katie breezed past without noticing the look of dismay on Jan's face.

It wasn't all right. A fiver was about all Jan had in the world just then without dipping into his very small bank balance.

"Right," he said, apparently agreeing. "See you later!"

They were all assembled when he returned from his session in the library and a lunch of beans on toast in the cafeteria. He could have had a snack with the gang in the Kelham's kitchen, but he had no supplies and was increasingly embarrassed at eating theirs.

"Ach – here you are finally," Claire greeted him. She didn't look directly at him, but chattered on nervously. "We're just trying to sort out some old clothes for Nikki's guy."

"Maybe you can sort out a few for me also," joked Jan. But then he suddenly remembered the baggy blue tracksuit. "Wait," he commanded. "I have something."

He darted upstairs and was soon back, carrying the terrible tracksuit.

"Is this useful?" he asked Nikki.

"Oh, it's just right," she said. "It'll be easy to sew up the trouser ends and sleeves, then I'll stuff it with straw..."

"Stuff it well, stick a pumpkin on top and it'll look like Derek Waterson," suggested Barbara.

Everyone laughed. Mr Waterson was the senior executive of Brassington Royal Hospital Trust Inc.

"Oh, yes," urged Katie. "You'll get a pumpkin from the kitchen; there's plenty left from Hallowe'en."

Nikki beamed; she didn't often stay at Kelham's at the weekends and was obviously enjoying herself. She looked unusually happy, Jan suddenly realized, in spite of the fact that she was on placement in the

Hospice. Obviously coping better than he was!

"Don't forget the straw," she ordered. "I'll see you all later, when I've done some work on the guy."

The others piled into the janitor's open truck, Barbara and Katie squashed up inside the cab with Nick, leaving Jan and Claire to ride outside.

"So you two can keep each other warm," teased Katie.

But they didn't. They sat on the floor of the truck, side by side but not really together. Jan knew Claire was waiting for him to make the first move, knew he owed it to her at least to hold her hand, put an arm around her shoulders. But he couldn't. It was as though a glass barrier was keeping them apart. The truck rattled and shook up the drive and round the back of the main hospital to the workshops. Jan sat back, closed his eyes and let his head bang loosely on the side of the truck. Suddenly he felt so weary...

"What is it?" He suddenly shook himself awake. "Lie down, Tanya," he ordered Claire roughly.

"What?" She looked at him, aghast.

Jan gulped. "Sorry," he said. "I must have fallen asleep..."

"And you wanted me to sleep with you?" asked Claire, with irony in her voice.

Jan shook his head, bewildered. "What?" he asked.

"You told me to lie down," she reminded him.

"Ah, no – I was thinking it was dangerous; the

truck ride was like the journeys we took through Czerny after a raid…"

"And Tanya?"

"Tanya." He repeated the name thoughtfully. "Sister Radski … was a nurse at the hospital. Once," he added.

It was Claire who took *his* hand then, firmly.

"Come on," she said. "Let's build a fire that will blaze to the skies."

All afternoon they worked, collecting broken-down furniture, branches trimmed from the trees all round the grounds, huge piles of boxes and packaging, mountains of paper. Eventually they had it all piled up on rough grass at the back of the children's wing.

"Sister Thomas says we'll have to start early," Katie told them. "Or there'll be temperatures and tantrums before the fireworks."

"Yeah," Nick agreed. "Then we can get off to the pub afterwards."

Barbara looked up at the lowering grey sky. "Hope the rain keeps off," she said. "Or the fire will never light."

"That's why we left it until this afternoon," Katie explained. "The forecast isn't too bad – showers later – so if we get the fire going and the fireworks over by eight…"

"Right," said Nick. "Let's go and see how the guy's coming along."

* * *

Guy – "Derek Waterson" – Fawkes was in fine fettle. Nikki had chalked pinstripes down Jan's blue tracksuit and tucked a striped tea-towel in the open front, like a shirt. The pumpkin head was crowned with an old mop, quite remarkably like Mr Waterson's stringy grey hair. She'd even unearthed a battered briefcase for him to carry.

"From my car boot," she said, without explaining how it came to be in there, cracked and mouldering.

"He's marvellous!" said Barbara. "The lipstick suits him!"

"A pity we haven't got a St Ag's tie and pair of glasses," said Katie. "Very symbolic – burning the old St Ag's, peering through the smoke into the future..."

"I have one," said Jan.

"What? A future?" teased Katie.

"A hospital tie."

"What on earth for?" asked Nick.

"Issued with my clothing when I was sent here," Jan explained. "It must have been on the list."

For a moment the others were silent. A hospital tie was on their lists too, but each of them, for varied reasons, had ignored the suggestion. Yet Jan had no choice; he hadn't even bought his own gear. "Issued," he'd said. And the Kelhamites suddenly felt sad for him.

"Well, thanks, Jan. That's wonderful," said Nikki

warmly. "It will be just the right finishing touch – though I doubt the children will notice the symbolism," she added to Katie.

"And I've got a spare pair of glasses," Nick offered.

"You?" asked Katie. "But you don't wear glasses."

"Not now lenses are so good," he grinned. "Hang on." He ran lightly up the stairs, followed by Jan.

"Let's all go up and have a cup of tea," suggested Barbara. "I'm parched and filthy after all that dust."

Over tea they decided that the guy was so brilliant he should make an entrance – on the janitor's truck.

"Nick can take us round the main drive." Katie was ready to produce the show, as usual. "The rest of us will sit in the back with sparklers. You can hold Derek on your knee, Jan."

Jan opened his mouth to protest. He had no intention of wasting his last fiver on a bonfire party which he was sure he'd hate. But looking round at the eager faces of his friends, he knew he couldn't refuse, even if it meant beans on toast every day next week.

So at seven o'clock the strange procession set off. Nick had rigged up a lantern at the back of the cab, where Jan sat with "Derek" on his knee, now complete with glasses and tie and looking, in the dim light, almost too good to be true.

"I'll bet there's plenty of people who'd be glad if it really was Mr Derek-Management-Waterson," commented Barbara, brandishing her sparkler like a weapon.

Everyone laughed – except Jan, who shuddered at the idea of anyone being caught on a burning heap.

As they approached the back of the children's wing a great cheer went up. Those patients who were mobile were out on the balconies; bed-patients were ranged along the big windows at the end of the ward. The lights blazed out behind them and they each waved a sparkler in greeting.

Nick pulled up and got out of the cab.

"Come on, let's be having him," he said to Jan, who passed the guy to him and picked up the folding ladder they had in the back of the truck.

Once they'd propped the ladder safely up the bonfire, Jan stood aside, assuming that Nick would take the guy up. But Nick held back.

"Up you go!" he said to Jan. "I'll pass the body up to you when you're halfway there; you can just drag it after that." He turned to fuss about with the guy's clothing.

Jan was surprised. Could it be that Nick Bone – mature, sensible, strong, healthy – was nervous of climbing a ladder? Coming from the mountains, where he'd walked and climbed all summer and skied all winter, Jan had no fear of heights. He scaled the ladder with ease, leant down to grab the guy from Nick, who was only a few rungs up, and moved on to the top, dragging the body after him. He set the guy up in the broken chair they'd saved for him, then slid down, fireman-style, the children's cheers ringing out all round him.

"Very impressive," said Nick tersely. "Now let's get this fire going."

This was the moment Jan had been dreading, but he'd reckoned without the damp English climate. Soon he was so intent on lifting bits of reluctantly smouldering wood from one part of the fire to the other in an attempt to get it to burn regularly that he totally forgot about the blazing fires of the war at home. Forgot, too, to be awkward with Claire, who was also working on getting the blaze going.

With hands and faces filthy, clothes stinking, they stood watching the first flames begin to curl upwards through the pile, urged on by another cheer from the children.

"At last," said Claire, coughing through the smoke. "Though I don't know why you and I should be helping to celebrate the death of a Catholic."

"It is strange," Jan agreed. "The English – they have no carnival, no saints' days, and yet they have this funny festival called … what is it called?"

"Bonfire Night," Claire told him.

"There you are, you see," said Jan.

"Where am I?" asked Claire. And Jan knew she meant more than her words.

"It just proves that the English are odd," he went on, not choosing to take her up on any deep meaning. "They have only one bonfire in the whole year so it does not need a special name."

Claire moved up close and they stood together in the glow of the fire.

"You have this celebration in Ireland?" he asked.

She shook her head. "Not in the South. We're not British, you know."

"A foreigner," said Jan softly. It was one of the things they had in common; he'd often called her his little foreigner. Now he looked down into her smoke-smudged face and for a moment he wanted to hold her close, tell her about his fears, explain why he was keeping so much apart...

They moved together, clung to each other and, silhouetted against the red glow, they kissed and the watching children cheered.

He would do it, he decided, tonight. He would explain to her about needing to keep running, to keep quiet, to keep working. She'd understand. Claire was a warm, intelligent girl. He turned to her again.

Suddenly there was a zipping, swooshing sound, as if the air was being sucked upwards into the sky.

Then a loud bang, followed by lots of small cracks like rifle shots. From the windows, children shouted and screamed in mock fright.

And Jan Buczowski crumpled to the ground.

Chapter 8

His first thought was to scramble up in the hope that nobody had seen him. But even as he moved his head the nausea hit him. And as for getting to his feet – well, the earth was heaving and shifting beneath them. He groaned and turned his face into the grass, the pops and bangs of the fireworks, the roar and the cracks of the bonfire filling his ears, his brain, his head. Grabbing tufts of grass in both hands, he clung on to the earth.

"Jan, are you all right?" Claire was bending over him, anxious as ever.

Jan took a deep, shuddering breath. "I must have slipped," he said, laughing shakily.

"But we weren't even moving."

He opened his mouth to reply and suddenly felt

too exhausted. It really didn't matter. Nothing mattered.

"Will I help you to get up?" asked Claire.

He didn't reply.

"Jan, you can't just lie there all night! Come on, let me help you."

He felt her gently shift his shoulders, knew she was turning him over easily, expertly. Claire was a good nurse, he reflected, and even in the firelight she'd notice...

"Jan, your face is all wet. You're crying!" she exclaimed, her voice breaking. "Oh, Jan, are you hurt?"

He began to breathe quickly now, trying to batten down the panic. Hurt? Yes, that was the way. If only he'd hurt his ankle as he fell...

"My foot," he said, pointing downwards. Claire's hands moved around his ankle firmly, professionally. Jan groaned as if in pain, though it was the prospect of humiliation that worried him.

"That's not swollen," said Claire. Tentatively she pushed his foot to the left, then the right. Jan was too tired even to protest and he certainly didn't know how to act a broken ankle. "There's full rotation," she went on. "Maybe you just bruised it as you fell."

He could tell from her voice she didn't believe for a moment in the sprained ankle.

"Come on, Jan – you really must move," she

urged with just the slightest touch of impatience in her voice. "It's dangerous so close to the fire and all. Here – up we go!"

Taken by surprise, he allowed himself to be pulled into a sitting position. Silently, Claire handed him a handkerchief and he mopped his wet, muddy face. With shaking hands, he noted with clinical interest; and he was very, very cold.

"Could you stand up now?" Claire asked.

Not trusting himself to speak, Jan shook his head. He could feel her sizing him up, working out the best way to get him to his feet. Thankfully, he remembered how small and light she was. No matter how skilfully she supported him, she'd never get him upright.

"I'll get Nick," she said. "You'll be all right for a moment. Just sit still."

And before he could protest, she was gone. And he didn't really mind, was quite relieved to be left alone in the glow of the fire. His head began to nod, his shoulders sagged, he felt so sleepy...

A spray of rockets whooshed up in the sky and fountains of sparks fell with a whistling, whining noise. As if galvanized by the sound, Jan scrambled to his feet, swaying slightly, but upright and walking – away from the fire, the fireworks, Claire...

He was on the running track, feet pounding, working hard, keeping moving, but the panic stayed with him. He forced his leaden legs forwards – one, two, one, two, faster, faster, up the hill towards the spinney.

It was as if he were running home, he thought, evening lectures ended, supper calling – across the river and into the trees, up the hill to the house where he'd lived all his life until the war came.

And here are the stone steps leading up to the terrace. Not enough steps, though; the house is high above the river and flights of steps rise up through the garden. Where had they all gone to? He paused for a moment and looked back through the darkness, catching a glimpse of mist rising over the grounds and the glow of the children's bonfire over the hill. The glow of burning, he thought, over the river; had the tanks arrived?

He pushed on upwards, walking now, not running, up the steps, through the darkness, wondering why there were no lights. His grandmother, Granya, always left the terrace light on for him; perhaps there was no electricity again? He pushed past the wet bushes and stepped on to the terrace.

Suddenly orange light flooded the whole building and Jan's steps faltered. He stood blinking, trying to understand. Was it an explosion? Had they bombed the house? Where were his parents? He ran forwards and pushed at the glass door. It didn't move. Frantically he snatched at the handle, shaking the glass.

And now his ears were filled with the shattering sound of screaming sirens. Jan crouched low, holding on to his head as if it would burst. Sirens! Another attack on Czerny! He must get back over the river to the hospital, to the patients. He stood now, reeling back from the lights and the noise, and fell once more, this time on to concrete.

"Well, well, well! I never expected to see you in here of a Sunday, lad. Certainly not in bed!"

Jan opened his eyes and saw Geoff, towering over him for once.

"Aye, that's it – wake up. Had a good night, did you?"

Jan frowned. Night – that was what he remembered. Night and fire and bangs…

"Is it over?" he asked.

Geoff nodded. "Bonfire night's over, if that's what upset you," he said. "Breaking and entering's over, if that's what you were doing." Then, gently, "But I don't think your nightmare's over yet, not by a long chalk."

Jan didn't even try to work out the meaning of that. He sighed, leaned back on his pillow, and closed his eyes.

"I'll send you some tea," said Geoff.

He woke up to find Karen sitting beside the bed, reading a magazine and sipping from Geoff's mug.

"Panda," said Jan.

"No, it's just the way I do my eyes," grinned Karen. "Now sit yourself up and drink this." She didn't ask him whether he wanted the tea, merely shoved the mug into his shaking hand and pushed a pillow up behind his head.

She didn't ask how he was feeling either. She just went on sipping and reading. So Jan sipped too, relishing the feel of the warm, sweet tea as it sluiced the metallic taste away from his mouth.

"Have I been drinking?" he wondered aloud.

Karen looked up. "In here?" she asked. "Chance'd be a fine thing!" She put her magazine down. "Mind you, I thought you had been, last night."

"Last night?" Jan's mind edged away from thoughts of last night.

"Yeah – when the alarm went. Found you all of a heap on the terrace. Thought you'd been out on the binge. Bit early, mind, but I know you medics have your own supplies."

"Binge?"

She nodded. "Yeah – you know, some sort of celebration. A few beers, a few vodkas, out with the lads…"

Jan shook his head. "With the children," he said. "It was the children's bongfire…"

"Yeah, apparently. That's where you were last seen. Caused no end of a rumpus searching the grounds for you."

"I was lost?" he asked, interested.

"Missing," she corrected. "You went missing. Until you set our alarm off. Hey, it was great – security guards, dogs ... better than Saturday night telly, I can tell you. Geoff had to be fetched; it was him who had you brought in here. They were all for sending you to casualty once I'd identified you. Good job I knew you, eh?"

"Good job," agreed Jan. "I'm sorry for all the – er – rum-pus."

Karen laughed as she took his empty mug. "Nah! It was good entertainment. I was going to go out for an hour but you saved me the money." She leaned behind and pushed his pillow down. "Sleepy-byes," she said. "I'm going to take Martin for his run – woof, woof!"

Jan drifted off once more, smiling this time.

The day went by in a blur of sleep and dreams and awakenings which passed like dreams. The Kelhamites drifted through, though he couldn't remember who'd been when, and it didn't seem to matter anyway. Nick brought his things over – all in one small suitcase – and the girls came with gifts: fruit and magazines and Grandma Robinson's home-made cookies. So he knew they'd been to see him, had a vague recollection of snatches of conversation, and a vague sense of unease whenever he thought of Claire.

It was as if they were ghosts from some previous existence, he thought. Geoff was more real to him than his friends from Kelham's. So was Karen – and Martin, who sat in silent vigil by his bedside late into the night. Martin rarely spoke, never smiled, only occasionally glanced in the direction of the bed, yet whenever he woke, Jan found comfort in the boy's presence.

Most of the time he slept, and in his dreams he was back home. Not in the shattered hospital in Czerny, but home as it used to be, on the hill above the river, with Granya waiting at the top of the steps. His parents were nowhere to be seen, but it didn't seem to matter. Nothing mattered…

He awoke with a jump next morning and lay listening to the thud-thud of trainers and the single bang on each door as someone came down the corridor. The steps hesitated outside his door, the knocking was subdued.

"Jan! You running?" It was Karen. "Jan? Come on! Twice round the spinney, last one home's a dwork."

A what? thought Jan, automatically reaching out for his notebook. But his hand dropped even before it reached his locker; it didn't matter now. He pulled the quilt up over his face and lay quite still, waiting for the footsteps to continue.

When they did, he sat up, pulled back the

curtains and looked out at the grey drizzle. Tears fell unheeded down his cheeks, off his chin, though he couldn't think why they should; he wasn't consciously weeping, wasn't even unhappy. Wasn't anything. He slid back on his pillows and slept.

Again the knocking awoke him, but this time it was different – firmer, sharper. The door opened and Geoff came in.

"You missed the run this morning, Jan," he announced, ignoring the inert figure in bed. "Still, you've just got time for a bit of breakfast, then I'll see you in my office at nine. Right?"

Shocked into action, Jan sat upright, wide-eyed. "I can't," he said.

"What do you mean?" asked Geoff sharply.

"I can't do those things – go to breakfast, to your office."

"Why not?" Geoff looked genuinely surprised. "You'll make it in time if you get a move on."

"No, I don't mean there's no time. I mean I can't … can't…" Jan's voice trailed miserably off.

"Can't what?" Geoff asked, gently persisting.

Jan gave a shuddering sigh. "I can't get up," he muttered.

"I see." Geoff looked at him thoughtfully. "Well, your injuries were quite slight – that cut on your arm, a few bruises. Maybe it was the bump on your head. Shall I send you for an X-ray?"

Jan shook his head. "Not cuts and bruises," he whispered. "Not the bump on the head."

"So what is it that's stopping you getting out of bed?" Geoff prompted.

There was a pause. Jan looked at Geoff; surely the man could see what was wrong? He was a qualified nurse, wasn't he? And his specialism was Mental Health?

"You know, Jan, by rights you should have reported for duty half an hour ago," Geoff pointed out mildly.

"For duty?" Jan was horrified. How could he be expected to go on duty, to help the patients when he himself was…

"I'm too ill," he said.

"Ah, now we're getting somewhere." Geoff nodded. "Where are you ill?"

Jan hesitated. He felt terrible in a general sort of way, but he couldn't begin to describe any specific symptom.

"I have a headache," he said, though he hadn't.

"I'm not surprised," Geoff said. "It's this over-heated building. You should have come out for a run – that would've cleared your head."

"I couldn't run," said Jan. "I am too tired – terribly, terribly tired."

Geoff nodded, apparently sympathetic. "You're all the same, you students," he said. "So used to sitting on your bum all day, the first week on placement knocks you out."

Jan couldn't believe what he was hearing. He'd seen himself in the bathroom mirror, knew he looked ghastly – sheet-white, gaunt, patches under his eyes black as bruises. Why couldn't Geoff see this?

"I *am* ill," he said, quite loudly this time.

"How?" Geoff repeated.

Tears welled up from Jan's eyes; swallowing a sob, he pointed to himself. "In here," he gasped, pounding his chest. "And here," pointing to his head. "I am so sick and so tired I can't get up." His head dropped, his whole body sagged, his hands dropped down on to the bed and he felt the tears drip down his pyjama jacket. "Don't you understand?" he asked.

"Aye, lad, I understand." Geoff leaned over and patted Jan's thin shoulder gently. "Point is, do you?"

There was a long silence, then Jan looked up, wiped his wet face, and nodded. "Yes," he said. "I understand that I am ill inside myself, in my soul, mayhaps." He took a deep, shaky breath. "Mentally ill," he said. And he sat back with something like relief.

"Well, now you've admitted it, you're on your way to getting better." Geoff smiled and nodded at him thoughtfully for a moment. "So, you're in a funny old position in this department, aren't you?"

he said. "No longer a student nurse – more a patient." He laughed. "What are we going to do with you?" he asked.

"I hope you're going to make me better," said Jan, smiling painfully.

"Nay, lad, we can't do that. I've told you – in the end that's up to you." He turned to the door. "And Dr Hammond, of course. That's why I want you in my office at nine o'clock. Dr Hammond's popping in to have a chat with you – right?"

He stared at Jan. Jan stared back then slowly, hesitantly, he nodded.

"I will come," he said.

Chapter 9

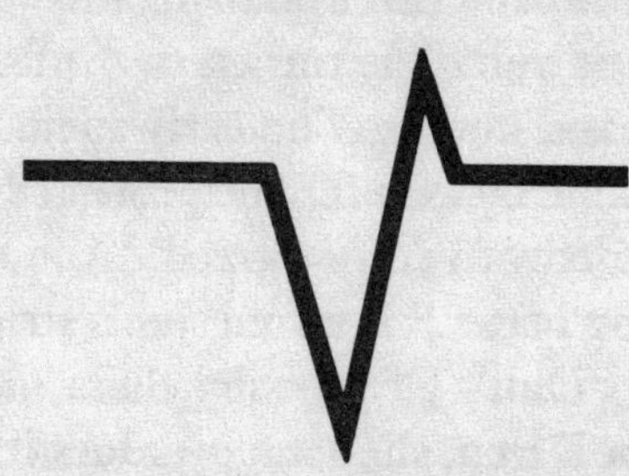

And so Jan was transformed from student nurse to hospital patient – or so he thought. Dr Hammond prescribed largactil, Geoff prescribed rest and quiet and Karen provided the back-up service. It seemed to Jan that all he had to do was to keep on taking the pills, ask Karen to make the occasional coffee, and shut himself up in his room alone, dozing and dreaming day and night.

But he soon found there was a price to pay.

"You can take the run tomorrow," Geoff told him towards the end of the week. "I'm off."

"Off where?" Jan asked.

"Off – you know, as in 'day off'." I came in last Saturday night, worked over Sunday, didn't I?"

Jan shook his head; he couldn't remember last Sunday – or even last night. Didn't want to.

"Doug Bellamy's on but he won't take the run. Plays it by the book, does our Doug." Geoff leaned over and patted Jan's back. "So, it's up to you, lad."

Jan stared stonily out of the window. "I can't."

Geoff ignored him. "We've just got a nice little group going now – don't want to lose 'em. They soon get out of the habit, you know – miss a couple of mornings and never get up early again."

Jan sighed. "But I am ill," he protested.

Geoff nodded. "Aye," he agreed. "And this is one way of getting better." Ignoring Jan's stricken face, he went on, "Don't go pressing them too much – especially not Karen; she soon overdoes it. Martin's your pace-maker – slow but steady, could keep on for hours."

"I can't go," Jan turned his back on Geoff.

Geoff said nothing and he never moved. Eventually Jan turned over to see what he was doing. He was sitting in the single armchair, apparently dozing, but as Jan sat up his eyes opened.

"I was thinking," he said, "that if you go on working with the group, living here for a bit but keeping all your notes for your assignment, you could pass this placement with flying colours."

"Colours?"

"Aye – you know, as in flags."

Jan frowned. "I don't understand," he said.

"Right, I'll explain the reference; where's your notebook?"

Jan looked vaguely round. He had no idea where the notebook was; he hadn't even noticed a new word for days.

But Geoff flipped through all the papers on the dressing-table and soon came up with the little red book. Further search revealed a pencil.

"Now then, 'flying colours'," he said. "Ready?"

Jan blinked at the white page, took the pencil in his shaking fingers, and began laboriously to write as Geoff expanded on the theme of flags and warfare as if Jan was a military student, not a nurse. Jan looked at the wobbly letters on the page and wondered why he himself was bothering. Why Geoff was bothering…

Nevertheless, he went on writing, and drawing the little flags as Geoff described them, and he noticed his hand grow steadier, his interest ever so slightly roused. Ah – occupational therapy – that's what Geoff was up to! Jan glared at him and stopped writing.

But before he could protest he was interrupted by a knock on the door.

Head bowed, Jan quickly turned his attention to his notebook.

"Go on," urged Geoff. "Tell 'em to come in."

Jan looked round the small room, made even smaller with Geoff's bulk spreading over the armchair, his legs sprawled out, filling the only space.

"There is no room," he pointed out.

"That's all right – I'm just leaving." Geoff stood up. "Go on," he said again. "It's your room – I can't invite anybody in."

Jan sighed. "Come in," he muttered, unwelcoming. After all that therapy nonsense from Geoff, he really didn't feel he could face another visitor.

Especially not Claire Donovan.

"Oh, I'm very sorry," she said, pausing in the doorway. "I didn't realize you were busy."

Jan looked helplessly at Geoff, but he moved over to the door.

"Nay, lass, I'm just off." He turned and grinned at Jan. "See you Monday," he said. "And don't forget that run."

He left a space behind him – a silence too. Jan slumped back on his pillows, avoiding Claire's eyes, as she went across to sit down.

"How are you feeling?" she asked.

Jan shrugged.

"Are you feeling better than you did last weekend?" she persisted.

"I don't know," he said, truthfully. He didn't want to remember how he'd felt last weekend.

There was a pause – a long pause. Jan stared at the wall at the end of the bed, Claire fiddled with the plastic bag on her lap.

"I'm sorry I didn't come to see you sooner," she said eventually.

"It is all right," Jan assured her. It was more than that, he reflected; it was quite a relief.

"I thought maybe you needed a breathing space," Claire went on, her voice so quiet and low that he had to strain to hear it. "You see, in some way I feel responsible for your … breakdown."

She'd said it aloud. It was the first time Jan had heard his condition labelled. Dr Hammond was very careful to avoid labels – "stress", he'd called it, and something called "PTS", which, he'd explained, often happened to people who'd come through a particularly bad experience. "Post-traumatic Syndrome"; Jan recalled the words, took comfort in them.

"It is stress," he said coldly to Claire. "We do not use the word 'breakdown' here."

Claire flushed. "I'm sorry," she said.

"And you are not responsible," he went on. "It is stress from the battles, from leaving my country, my home, my…" "Family," he wanted to add, but dared not. Even to think of them would start up the tears. "You must not blame yourself," he added rather severely. Then, to his own surprise, he said, "I am getting better now."

"Good." Claire looked at him doubtfully and he knew she was noticing his black-ringed eyes, his haggard face, his hands, trembling again already. Swiftly he shoved them under the covers and grasped one in the other, to hold them still.

"Well, I am better than last weekend," he assured Claire, making a ghastly attempt to smile. "So much better that tomorrow I am in charge of the early morning run." Again, the words took him by surprise.

"Good," said Claire doubtfully. "So when are you coming back?"

The smile collapsed. Why was everyone so keen for him to go back to where he didn't want to be?

"Back?" he asked, playing for time. "Back where?"

"To Kelham's, of course," she said. "To your friends."

Jan didn't answer. It seemed to him that Kelham's and The Six were part of a different existence now. They might have been on another planet. He couldn't even imagine himself taking the journey across the grounds. In some ways Czerny seemed closer.

"I must stay here," he muttered.

"As a patient?" Claire asked, sharply. "Or as a nurse?"

There was no answer to that. Jan shrugged and turned away from her.

Claire took a deep breath. "You see, I do feel responsible. I think your – er – trouble started over in Donegal. Maybe it was the flight that triggered off something, or perhaps it was just the holiday that did it – relaxing and all..."

"Ah, so you are a psychiatrist?" Jan sneered.

"No, I'm not," Claire said quietly, and Jan immediately felt guilty. "But I have been thinking, Jan, about you – about us." She paused, as if giving him the opportunity to interrupt. He didn't, so she went on. "You may be right to stay over here for a while, whatever your role. Things are always hectic over at Kelham's; we're not the most restful company, I know." She smiled. "And I think that's what you're needing now, Jan – a rest – from us all."

Silence. Jan could hear the spatter of rain on the window, the steady hum of the central heating system, and far away, down the corridor, a familiar "toc-toc-toc" of heavy rubber boots.

"So you see," Claire stood up, "you mustn't be worrying about me – about us. We'll just take a little holiday from each other – see how things are when you're feeling better."

She leaned over the bed to look into his eyes. And all the time he was aware of the footsteps getting closer.

"Bye, love," said Claire. She took his hand and held it up to her face. "When – if – you want to see me, just tell one of the others."

Jan could scarcely breathe. When the knock came at the door, he couldn't even call an answer.

"Jan? You there, love?" Karen's voice sounded clearly through the door, cheerful and chirpy as it always was when she was on a high.

Jan sat up and pulled his hand away from Claire. "Come in!" he called brightly.

She stood in the doorway, a vision of leather and metal, her short, blonde spikes around her head like a halo.

"Hi!" she lifted a hand to Claire. "You one of his nursing friends?"

"Yes, I am," said Claire, though she was still looking at Jan. "Just one of his nursing friends," she said. And then she turned away, pushed past Karen and was gone.

"Wow!" Karen whistled. "Did I interrupt something?"

She wasn't nearly so bright and bumptious next morning, Jan observed. Nobody was. Now he realized why they were so silent on the runs: merely getting out of bed used up most of their energy and they had none left for talking. When Martin had banged on his door that morning, Jan had turned his face into his pillow and groaned. He couldn't get up, he told himself – hadn't the strength to move off the bed, never mind run along the track. But Martin had persisted and Jan, afraid he would awaken the whole corridor, struggled into his track-suit and out to the foyer where half a dozen runners awaited him.

And now they were spread out along the track – Karen leading, pressing hard as usual, though she looked as if she'd hardly slept all night, Martin midfield, staring straight ahead, pushing one foot in front of the other, one-two, one-two...

From the end of the line, Jan watched and remembered that feeling of being on automatic pilot. The feeling he'd had when he'd run to the Mental Health Unit, away from the fire and the bangs of the fireworks. The feeling he'd experienced at Czerny Hospital, when casualties were arriving every second and the throb of heavy gunfire echoed relentlessly from the hills above the town. Jan closed his eyes for a second, as if to wash away the memories.

And opened them sharpish as a cry went out ahead. Putting on a spurt, he caught up with a cluster of people by the copse.

"Karen's done a runner," announced Alan, the oldest in the group.

"Again," added Margaret, jogging from foot to foot. "Shall we go and get her?" she added with relish.

"We'd never catch up," said Alan.

Jan could feel his heart racing, the saliva rising in his mouth, the hint of nausea edging up from his stomach. Oh God, not now! Doug Bellamy had made it very obvious that he wasn't happy with Jan's dual role on the unit.

"So what are you, then?" he'd asked, apparently innocently. "A nurse off sick or a fit patient?"

Jan had refused to answer then, but now he realized that if he didn't cope with this crisis, he'd soon be classified – in Doug's mind at least – as an unfit patient. Or, worse, as a mentally sick nurse, bundled back into the main hospital. And suddenly he knew he didn't want either label.

"Which way?" he asked, addressing Martin, who pointed off the track and into the woods.

Jan hesitated. None of this group needed to be kept under supervision; Alan, for example, often came out running alone, as did Martin. But some of the patients were at their worst first thing, so it was accepted that they should be accompanied by someone from the staff – even someone as lowly as Jan. Doug Bellamy had expressed his doubts about Jan leading the run as soon as he'd arrived on duty that morning. If Jan sent them back unaccompanied...

On the other hand, it was accepted that Karen was prone to doing a runner – and to harming herself in all sorts of ways. And yet, when she'd last run away from him up at the hospital, it was only to have a cigarette.

"We'll take the path up through the woods," he said decisively. "You take the lead, Martin – as fast as you like. And everyone will smell."

There was a pause and Jan was aware of puzzled faces turning to him. He sniffed.

"Like so," he explained. "Karen will be smoking

somewhere, I think."

"Ah! You mean we're on the scent," said Alan. And everyone laughed, partly at the joke, but mainly, Jan reflected, with relief. Relief at what? At having someone to take decisions? Well, he knew how they felt – wished he had someone to take a few decisions for him. No time now though.

"Come on, then," he said. "Off you go, Martin."

They ran on steadily, not fast, sniffing the air and smiling at each other – the first time Jan had seen them exchange any looks at all. And he understood now why they didn't, why they rarely communicated. The blackness, the blankness, the utter exhaustion and the sleepless nights left them without interest in anyone or anything other than their illness. It was all-consuming.

But this little crisis had brought them together, given them an aim in common, quite apart from their illness and their treatments. Jan jogged alongside Margaret and noticed that his symptoms of panic had subsided now. He almost smiled.

But a shout up ahead made him put on speed. Martin was at an intersection where a narrow track led deep into the undergrowth. His head was held unusually high, his nose in the air – obviously sniffing – and he was pointing, almost animatedly, into the bushes.

He made no attempt to speak, however, when Jan joined him. Not that there was any need: the smell of cigarette smoke overlay the dank scent of rotting vegetation.

"Karen!" Jan called. "Karen, you have led us off the track; now come and lead us home again."

No answer. The others came up now, standing in a silent group around him.

"Karen," Jan tried again. "We must get back; Doug Bellamy will not be pleased with me if we are late." Blackmail, he thought, grimly, that's what this is. He knew Karen was fond of him; she'd want to protect him from Doug Bellamy's wrath.

And he was right – there was a response. Not an actual answer, more a rustling in the bushes and a slight sound – a whimper, perhaps?

Martin looked a question at Jan, who nodded, and they both pushed off the path and into the dense undergrowth. Jan felt the brambles dragging at his tracksuit, ripping his hands, tangling in his hair, and yet he didn't care. It was as if the effort of battling with the brambles was creating energy within him. Grunting, he thrust a fist through the prickly barrier towards the light and almost fell over Karen as she crouched in a sudden clearing.

"Come on, Karen!" Jan commanded. "You should not rest in the middle of running; it is bad for the circulation."

But she didn't move. Couldn't move, he realized.

"Are you hurt?" he asked. He was suddenly reminded of a similar situation, with himself prone on grass, Claire asking the same question as she bent to examine his ankle.

Karen lifted her head and grimaced with pain as he gently worked the right foot.

"Never mind that – find my lighter," she commanded.

Martin had joined them now. He reached out to lift Karen up but she waved him away.

"Go and look for my lighter," she told him. "I dropped it when I fell over that damned root."

Martin obediently turned his attention to the grassy tussocks around them. Jan, meanwhile, had loosened the lace of Karen's trainer. He tried to ease it off.

"Ooooh!" she gasped. "Just leave it alone."

Jan looked down at her; she was very white now, her face creased with pain and shock. And it was a relief to know that she had something physically wrong with her; dealing with injuries came easily to him.

"Here – wrap this round you." He took off his tracksuit top and put it on her shoulders. "Now, Martin and I will lift you – like a cradle, see?" He indicated with crossed hands. "Come on, Martin," he called.

Between them they lifted Karen on to her one good foot, then cradled her back through the path they'd left in the undergrowth. As soon as they emerged, the others came forward with murmurs of concern.

"Eeh, you've done it now, Karen," said Margaret. "You'll not be doing a runner for many a day now." But she smiled at the injured girl, and supported her bad leg so that it didn't drag painfully down.

"Alan, can you get close behind us; lift her a little under her arms, let her head rest against you," Jan commanded. "Now, are you comfortable, Karen?" He turned to look into her peaky little face.

Karen shook her head. "What about my lighter?" she demanded. "And the rest of my fags?"

Jan almost laughed at her – and then felt amazed by the urge. It was a long time since he'd wanted to laugh.

"Martin and I will come back to find them," he promised. "But now we must get you back to the unit and over to X-ray – pronto."

"I'll hold you to that," said Karen, rather faintly. She turned to look up at Jan and gave a great wink.

Jan couldn't help smiling back, taken by surprise by the surge of tenderness he suddenly felt for her. Not that Karen would notice – she'd fainted again.

"Let's go!" he ordered. He braced his shoulders and, nodding to the other two carriers, led the group back up the running track.

Chapter 10

"I shouldn't be spending too much time with Karen Shelford, if I were you, lad," Geoff said.

Startled, Jan looked up from the files he was checking. He was in Geoff's office, working on a tedious administrative job that he would have despised as "non-medical" a week ago. But now he enjoyed the steady routine and the silent, undemanding company of Geoff. He was feeling better, in a vaguely uneasy way, so long as he kept busy with simple, non-stressful tasks. And although Dr Hammond assured him that the anti-depressants would not start working for at least a week, he was already sleeping more peacefully.

And without consciously taking the decision, he had settled back into his role of student nurse again.

Nick brought his files and notes across, Nikki collected psychology books from the library and Katie, obviously puzzled as to why Claire always passed the job on to her, dashed in with assignment hand-outs.

So Jan's daily routine was becoming established: early morning run (without Karen, alas!), snack and coffee in the residents' kitchen, work on the computer for Nurse Hawley, a few admin jobs for Geoff – all very peaceful, very satisfactory. For the first time in weeks, Jan felt he had things under control.

He spread the files out on Geoff's desk, noting with pleasure that his hands were almost steady now.

"We are all spending much time with Karen, now she is stuck in the unit," he observed.

Karen's fall had resulted in an inflamed Achilles tendon; her leg was strapped up and she had to rest it.

"Couldn't even walk out of this place, never mind do a runner," she'd joked, holding court in the lounge all day. Even so, she was getting around on her crutches with remarkable speed and had queues of eager attendants ready to push the wheelchair across to the cafeteria at meal times.

But Jan preferred to see her alone in her room, partly because he knew she'd be feeling low, but mostly, he had to admit, because he wanted to be alone with her.

"She spent a lot of her time with me before her accident," he pointed out to Geoff.

"I know she did," Geoff agreed. "But that was different; she's free to visit who she likes, but you're part of the team. It doesn't do to get involved with a patient, you know." He looked closely at Jan, who flushed and bent over his work. "Any road up," Geoff went on, "you'll not be around so much yourself now you're feeling better."

"What?"

"It's time you were getting back to Kelham's," said Geoff.

Jan stared at him. "But … I am not ready for that," he protested.

Geoff shrugged. "And you never will be if you stay on here," he said. "Besides, I need the room."

There was no arguing with that; Jan went on with his filing in sullen silence.

"You can take this afternoon to move your stuff," Geoff offered. "Need a lift?"

Jan shook his head. "I have only my bag," he said. "I'll take it when I go off this evening." He hesitated. "After I've spent some time with Karen."

"I wouldn't do that." Geoff spoke gently. "You'll see plenty of her in the daytime – in your official capacity," he added firmly.

By the time he'd packed his bag – and three plastic carriers – Jan almost wished he'd taken up Geoff's offer of a lift. He couldn't believe how much stuff he'd acquired in little more than a week. He put Nick's portable CD/radio carefully back into its box and gathered up a dozen or more discs from the dressing table: dance music from Nick – not Jan's taste – and a couple of Clannad. His heart sank: they must be Claire's. Then there were Nikki's big art books, a box of cookies from Barbara and a whole bowlful of fruit – a collective offering organized by Katie. She'd delivered it only last Saturday, wide-eyed and curious.

"Claire says to let her know if there's anything you need," she said. "She's working in the library all morning," she added pointedly. They both knew that Jan usually helped Claire with her assignments.

Jan merely nodded, accepted the gifts and listened to the latest news from Kelham's with an air of detachment. It meant nothing to him just then; he could scarcely remember being there. It seemed to him that the Mental Health Unit was the best place on earth to be: safe, secure, with a regular routine and a gentle atmosphere. Kelham's was filled with bright talk and loud laughter – and Claire. What was he to do about Claire?

Gloomily he picked up his luggage and staggered out to the foyer.

"You're leaving us, then?" Margaret was sitting by the desk, rocking gently from side to side.

"I'll be back in the morning," said Jan, trying to sound cheerful.

"Aye." Margaret nodded more vigorously. "But you'll not be one of us then, will you?"

Jan looked at her helplessly. She was right, of course, but he didn't want to admit it.

"Will you take these into the kitchen?" He offered the bag in which the cookies and fruit were packed. "Tell everyone to help themselves."

She nodded into the carrier bag, delved in and produced the cookies.

"Thanks!" she said. "Just in time for afternoon tea. I'll go and put the kettle on." Clutching the bag to her, she scuttled off to the kitchen.

"I hope they all like spicy biscuits," said Barbara, standing by the open door.

Jan jumped guiltily. "Oh, I liked them very much," he assured her. "But I have to leave and there is so much to carry..." He surveyed the collection of plastic bags with dismay.

"Lucky I came over to see you, then," said Barbara. "Come on – you take the travel bag, I'll take the rest."

Jan looked back to the lounge, where he was sure Karen was lying on a sofa, leg propped up in front of her, Martin dancing attendance. Jan had planned to see her alone, to explain about losing his room, to assure her – of what?

"Ready?" Barbara asked, pausing at the main door.

"Yes," he said.

Jan had hoped to slip back into Kelham's unobserved. In the early evening most people would be in the cafeteria, having supper, or in the Medics' Mess, having a drink. Well, there would be coffee and milk up in the Kelhamites' kitchen and, with luck, a slice or two of bread to toast. He'd make do with that for supper; he was never hungry these days anyway. Then he'd sort out his room, turn in for the night, take a pill and hope to sleep until morning.

But he'd reckoned without Barbara.

"You look as though you could do with some decent food," she observed, as she put the carrier bags down in his room. "Soup's up in five minutes – made it yesterday."

Jan was about to protest, but she was already gone. He looked cautiously along the corridor. Nobody about. Apparently Barbara was the only one at home just then, and he felt he could face a bowl of her soup. He followed her into the kitchen.

"So, you're better now?" she asked, as she tipped the soup into a pan and lit the gas.

"Well, what is that word Katie uses," he smiled sadly, "when she means almost?"

"Oh, you mean 'nobbut just'." Barbara laughed. "You've got a good ear for languages, Jan."

"Well, I must thank all of you for that." Jan pulled

out a chair and sat at the table, leaning his head on his hands. "You have been so patient with me. I even think in English now. Soon I shall forget my own language." He smiled, though he wasn't joking.

"You mustn't do that," Barbara told him. "You'll need it again one day."

Slowly, sadly, Jan shook his head. There it was again, that suggestion that he'd go back. They didn't know what they were saying, these people who'd never experienced war. Nobody in their right mind would go back to what was left of Czerny.

"I hear on the news that things are settling down," Barbara said. She poured dark liquid, pungent and thick, into his bowl. "Bread?" she asked.

Jan nodded. "Settling down in Czerny?" he asked. "There is nothing left to settle, I think."

"Well, that's why I was on my way to see you." Barbara came and sat down beside Jan, her expression serious, yet filled with suppressed excitement. "You know my mother is a nurse – a midwife?"

Jan took a sip of the soup and nodded. "This is very good," he said. "I have not felt hungry for days, but this I can eat." He tore a piece of bread off and chewed vigorously. For once he could really taste what he was eating. "Mmmm!" he muttered, bending to inhale the aroma.

"Listen, Jan, this is very important," Barbara said. "Now, my family are Adventists – you understand?"

Jan stopped chewing, swallowed hard and stared at her.

"You understand the word Adventists?" she asked him.

"Oh, yes. They were in Czerny even when we left. They have – immunization?"

"*Immunity*," Barbara corrected. "Yes, that's right. They work with the aid agencies, delivering food packs, medical supplies – and letters." She brought the last word out with a flourish.

"Letters?" Jan's eyes opened wide.

Barbara nodded. "My mum's been on a mission to your country, trying to get food and clothes and blankets to the camps before they're cut off by the winter. I saw her just before she left and gave her your family's name and the address you mentioned ages ago. Was it your house or your grandma's?"

"We all lived there together," said Jan, thinking of the tall shuttered house above the river and waiting for the pang of pain that always accompanied the memory. But it never came; maybe the pills were beginning to work already.

"Well, they're all back home now. I talked to Mum on the phone last weekend; she sounded as high as she always does when she's been doing good works."

"They are very brave, very kind, the Adventists," said Jan.

"And very clever, some of us," laughed Barbara. She put a hand on his arm and looked straight into his eyes. "She found them – your family – way up in the mountains, away from the worst of the fighting. Hey – you never told us your mother's a doctor."

Jan sat rigid, upright, quite, quite still, his spoon in his hand. Barbara was right: he'd never spoken to anyone about his family, not even to Claire. And everyone, assuming he'd left them behind, maybe even lost them, avoided the topic.

"Yes, she was," he whispered.

"Still is," Barbara corrected him. "She's running a sort of refuge for the injured and an orphanage for all the stray kids. My mum was most impressed at the work they were doing – with so few resources too..."

For once, Jan wasn't interested in hospital organization.

"Go on," he urged. "What about Father – and Granya?"

"It's all in the letters. Mum brought them out and posted them on. I got them today. I was just bringing them over when I met you in the foyer." She smiled. "Thought you'd rather receive them somewhere more private."

The spoon clattered down into the soup. Jan buried his head in his hands and took deep, shaking breaths. Gently, Barbara put a package on the table in front of him. Gently, very gently, she leaned over and squeezed his shoulder.

"I was in two minds as to whether to deliver them right away, or to wait until you were feeling more – more together, you know?" she said softly. "But, well, I'm not qualified yet, but my nursing instinct tells me that losing touch with your country – and especially your family – is at the root of your depression." She sat back and looked at the bowed head. "Anyway, Ma assures me this is what you need – 'better than all the tryptophan in the world, Barbie-girl!' she says. And she's the greatest nurse I know, since my gran retired."

Jan lifted up his face, blinked rapidly to clear the tears from his eyes, and looked at the package in wonder. He put out a finger, touched it, brought it gently towards him, then in a sudden movement, grabbed it and clutched it to his chest. Barbara turned back to the sink, ignoring the harsh, dry sobs behind her. She made a mug of coffee, sifting two spoonfuls of sugar into it.

"Here," she said. "Take this to your room, and read your letters in peace." She put a hand under his elbow and, with surprising strength, almost lifted him out of his chair, guiding him along the corridor to his room. "I'll be around if you need me." Then, closing the door softly, she left him alone with his letters.

Chapter 11

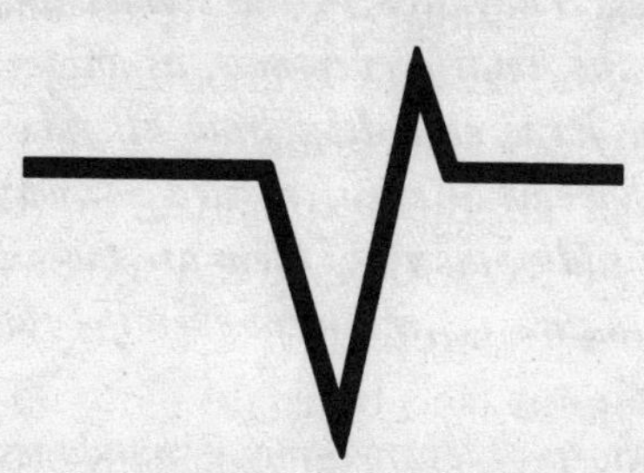

Vlada
Nov 5th

My dear Jan,

We were so relieved to hear from Serena Robinson that you are safe now. We knew about the evacuation from Czerny hospital but we thought you had been taken to Germany; indeed we were hoping you would be studying at one of the universities there. When Serena Robinson told me that you are a student nurse I laughed aloud. I think she was quite shocked, but then, she didn't know how hard you fought against a medical career. Well, this war has changed many things – including, it seems, your mind. Perhaps you will have the opportunity to change it again and study medicine later?

We were among the last to leave Czerny; we came straight up here to Granya's family house – you remember the holidays you used to have with Granya and Grandpa at the farm? We brought some refugees along with us, including many children who have lost their families. They live in the stables and barns or camp out in the fields – even now, as winter sets in. In the house we have casualties from all sides; many of them have hobbled – even crawled – away from the fighting and sadly, many of them are too weakened by the journey to survive treatment even if I could provide it.

We are short of everything – bandages, bedding, drugs, electricity, heating, food, clothing... Fortunately there is plenty of clean, fresh water, though it has to be brought up to the hospital in casks. I never thought to see your father driving a donkey up a mountainside!

I leave him to continue our story and send you my love, as always, dear, dear Jan. I am so proud and pleased that you have at last turned to medicine for your career. Perhaps this wretched war will have ended by the time you qualify as a doctor.

Mama

Jan sat at his desk, his mother's letter in his hand, though he stared blindly at the wall in front of him. He could see her now, tugging that stray strand of hair that always escaped from behind her ear, frowning slightly as she concentrated on a sick child or her notes. Funny – he couldn't imagine her without her white coat. Even through his tears, Jan smiled as he glanced once more at her letter; how typical that her first message for over a year should be concerned with medical details! Dear Mama, he thought, I wonder whether you've taken your white coat up to Vlada with you?

Sighing deeply, he turned to the next letter.

My dear son,

So – you have taken that longed-for trip to England without me after all! You remember how we dreamed of it one day, when the barriers were down? Well, they're down now and all the violent feelings, so long suppressed, are let loose. I can see no end to this war; there are too many private battles, too many personal revenges. Would you believe that they have taken all our papers, our passports, everything? So now we belong nowhere.

But perhaps it is good that we can start all over again from nothing. After all, that is what you are doing in England. I can only suppose you found the vocation for nursing while you were working in the hospital at Czerny. Well, you must do as you think fit, my boy. But if you wish to continue with your scientific studies, the University of Brassington has a fine reputation. Unfortunately we cannot offer you any financial help – we have not drawn a salary for over a year now and our little savings are dwindling daily.

Meanwhile the worst of the fighting is moving southwards and we are settling into the life of peasants. Luckily Granya still has her horticultural gift – we are rich in vegetables at least. I have two new careers now – both, of course, unpaid: headmaster of the local school and mayor of the district. And, you know, I am enjoying them both. I feel quite guilty when I thank the war for releasing me from the tedium of government committees.

And so the tides of war wash us clean of ambition; to survive is enough just now. When we meet again – as I trust we shall – we will see great changes in each other, my son, but my love for you remains as deep and constant as ever.

Your
Pappy

Now Jan gave up any pretence of holding back the tears. He admired and respected his mother, was even a little afraid of her, but he'd always loved his father deeply and his letter moved him in a way his mother's never could.

Oh, Pappy! Jan thought, between sniffs and sobs. If you could see me now – a cracked-up student nurse, too miserable to think about a new career, too much of a coward to return home to you...

He went over to the washbasin and sluiced away the tears. Granya's letter was brief, he noted with relief.

My dear Janni,

Serena Robinson brought us the best news ever. I knew in my heart that you were safe, but to know where you live and what you are doing, that is so much better. Now we can all talk of you and be happy with you.

But this war might go on for many years and I shall not. We must meet again very soon. I hear the coastal resorts are opening up again now and the tourists are being allowed in. You must come to one of the holiday resorts and then we can all meet again. I need a change of scene!

However you fix it, please come once more to your dear, dear,

Granya

Jan shook his head and smiled at this letter. His parents sent their love and advice, but Granya asked him to come back. Well, she had brought him up while his parents got on with their careers and she still thought of him as "Little Janni", bless her! He sat for a moment, feeling a great surge of love and warmth spread through him; now he knew they were safe he could get on with his life. And perhaps next year he might do as Granya asked, who knows?

But first he had to go and thank Barbara – and her mother; they had been so kind to arrange all this. He picked up the letters and found himself humming happily as he went down the corridor to the kitchen.

A figure was bent over the sink, silhouetted in the orange light from the car park below. Overtaken by a sudden joyful, grateful urge, he pulled her arm and began to dance round the table with her.

"Oh, thanks to you, Mrs Robinson..." he sang, misquoting the song he'd heard Barbara sing so often. "Janni loves you more than he can say. Yeah, yeah, yeah..."

He stopped suddenly as he realized his dancing partner was not Barbara Robinson.

It was Claire Donovan.

And she was a marvel. She sat Jan down at the kitchen table, filled up the big red pot with strong tea, fetched his pills, and sat in silence whilst he sipped tea and gazed at the letters spread before him as if drinking them too.

Claire tipped out two pills from the bottle and handed them to him.

"Oh, yes, thanks." Without looking at her he swallowed the pills, took another drink, and sighed deeply.

"I am so sorry," he said. "I have not always been right to you."

"I'm thinking perhaps we haven't been right for each other just lately," Claire said softly. "But I hope we are still friends?"

Jan took her hand, almost formally. "Very best friends," he said solemnly.

"Friends enough to share your news?" she asked.

"Of course," he said, handing the letters to her.

She shook her head. "I can't read your language," she protested.

"Oh, I am so stupid!" Jan struck his forehead. "I will translate."

"Wait!" Claire held up a hand. "I think the others are coming up now." She smiled and looked steadily at Jan as the sound of footsteps and excited chatter drew closer. "Could you bear to share them with us all?"

"You have all shared so much with me – food, money, clothes – you even shared your family, Claire. Now, everyone can share my joy." He looked up at her and smiled. "Call them in!"

It wasn't a glamorous celebration. In deference to Jan's drug regime and his reluctance to go out for a drink, Claire made fresh tea, Katie cut the last of the parkin, Nick made "odds-and-sods" sandwiches and Barbara emptied out the contents of the cookie tin.

Jan sat at the head of the kitchen table basking in the warmth of their friendship and feeling, for the first time, that he belonged here with them. The thought gave him courage.

"Now I will translate my letters," he announced.

They all sat very quiet while he read to them in a low, husky voice that just about managed not to crack. When he finished there was a pause whilst noses were blown and eyes wiped.

"Oh, Jan – I'm so glad my ma brought those letters back with her," said Barbara.

"I must write and thank her," Jan said. "She is a brave and wonderful lady."

"Brave and wonderful, yes," Barbara laughed. "But she's no lady – just an ordinary working nurse."

"A saint!" Jan exclaimed. "I saw the work the Adventists did in Czerny."

"Yeah, well, according to Ma, there's plenty left to do." Barbara turned to the others. "They're hoping to do another run before Christmas if they can get enough money together."

"Hey! We could help with that," Katie said eagerly. "We're good fundraisers." That was true: the Kelhamites had already had great success in fundraising both for St Ag's and for local charities.

"Do you not think people are a bit sick of giving us money?" Claire asked.

"And they're never very keen when there's no local angle," Nikki pointed out.

Barbara shrugged. "Don't you worry," she said. "They'll manage something. The Adventists' motto is 'The Lord will provide'."

"Well, I wish He would provide me with a ticket

home," murmured Jan. "Just to see Granya once more..."

There was a pause. Five pairs of eyes turned to the head of the table; thoughtful, pensive, calculating eyes.

"That's it!" cried Katie. "You *are* the local angle!"

"What?" Jan was startled.

"We raise funds for the Christmas convoy – and send you along with them!"

Jan stared at her, aghast. "I can't go back to Czerny," he said.

"Neither can they," Barbara told him. "It's too dangerous now. Ma says they're planning to drive up into the mountains where the refugee camps are."

"Vlada," murmured Jan. "Granya's farm." And for a moment he smelt the sweet, sickly scent of the cow barns and heard the wind sighing like the sea through the pines.

He stood up, lifting his mug high. "We will drink to Mrs Robinson's Christmas Convoy!" he declared. "And to the champion fundraisers – The Six!"

After the joys of celebrating – even with tea – Jan had the best night's sleep in months and found himself late for duty the next morning. Well, at least it wasn't a running morning, he consoled himself as he made his way across the hospital grounds. With any luck he could get himself installed in front of the computer and spend a quiet morning updating Nurse Hawley's drug lists.

But he'd reckoned without Karen. She was sitting waiting for him in the foyer, all set up in her wheelchair.

"You're late," she accused. "I've been waiting for you to come and push me across to breakfast."

"You never eat breakfast," Jan protested. "I'll get you coffee and toast from the kitchen here."

"Like hell!" Karen glared all round. "I'm pig-sick of being cooped up in here. I need a change of scene."

"A change of scene" – the very words Granya had used, the words she always used when she took Jan off to the farm for the summer. "The country food and fresh air will do us both good." Jan smiled; he could hear Granya's voice now, as if she was standing right there...

"...do you good," Karen was saying. "Are you listening to me, Jan?"

"No – sorry – what?" Jan stuttered.

"I told you that Dr Hammond would do you good, didn't I?" she repeated. "Still taking the pills, are you?"

Jan nodded. "I am feeling better," he admitted. But he knew that wasn't just the pills. Since yesterday he'd felt more secure, more rooted in the world, even though his family was still far away.

"Yeah, he's great, is Dr Hammond." Karen backed the chair off and looked hard at Jan. "Says I'll be able to leave before Christmas," she announced casually.

"Leave? You mean ... go home?"

Karen shrugged. "Half-way," she said.

"Half-way home?" Jan was puzzled. "Where is that?"

She laughed. "Not far away," she said. "It's a half-way home, as in half-way to getting better. A room in a house with somebody in charge in case you need help."

Jan looked at her thoughtfully. "We shall miss you, Karen," he said.

"Oh, no, you won't. I'll be back most days – Dr Hammond's clinic, therapy sessions – then there's my plaster to come off, followed by loads of physio. I'll be around a while yet." She looked at Jan, almost hopefully.

"I'm glad," he said.

"Glad enough to push me over to breakfast?" Karen grinned.

Jan hesitated, thinking of the queues, the clatter and the chatter in the cafeteria at that hour, and the sheer physical effort of shoving the wheelchair across to the main building.

"Come on!" Karen commanded, letting off the brake. "I'm ready!"

And perhaps I ought to be ready, Jan told himself.

I'll have to face the chatter and clatter of crowds when we're fundraising. And I'll have to be really fit to travel on the Christmas convoy. He moved behind Karen and grasped the handle of the wheelchair.

"Right!" he said. "Two all-day breakfasts, here we come!"

He set off across the foyer, through the glass door, out along the terrace and up the road at such a speed that Karen laughed and squealed and screamed all the way to the main entrance of St Ag's.

Epilogue

"All right at the back there?" the van driver called.

"All done." Jan slammed the double doors, turned the key, and made his way back up to the cab.

"Ready for the off?" The driver turned on the ignition.

Jan swung himself into the seat alongside the driver, clipped the belt on and settled back. "I'm ready, Serena," he said.

"Well, you can settle in for a long run," said Serena Robinson – driver just then, not midwife. "Apart from the break on the cross-channel ferry, you'll be living in that seat for three days."

"I don't mind," said Jan, grinning happily down at the traffic already jamming the suburbs in the weak dawn light.

"You can relax until we get over the last border," Serena promised. "I can manage a bit of French and Italian myself, but I'm certainly glad to let you take over with the Serbo-Croat."

Jan smiled. "Oh, it will be easy for me," he assured her. The easiest part of the whole business, he reflected; there had been so many obstacles to overcome.

In the first place, he was on placement at the Mental Health Unit until mid-December. Secondly, although his recovery was steady, it was slow; the panic attacks still hit him if he was over-tired and the depression was always there when he first woke. So even if the Kelhamites raised the funds for the Christmas convoy, Jan always had doubts as to whether they'd take a mental wreck along.

Serena Robinson, apparently, had no such doubts. Indeed, she made it a condition of accepting the funds. And Sister Thomas arranged his sick leave, Geoff Huckthwaite filled in a glowing placement report so that he wouldn't have to repeat the missing two weeks, and Claire's father sent a fantastically generous cheque, together with a vanload of canned food, which he claimed was what Jan would have eaten over Christmas in Ireland.

So many people had given so generously, Jan reflected. It was as if they felt responsible for the mad things that were happening in his country. A year ago, when he'd first arrived in England, he'd felt he belonged nowhere, to no one. Now, it seemed, he belonged all over the place, to everyone.

And in the frantic weeks of fund-raising he was "all over the place". The Kelhamites ran folk evenings in the Medics' Mess, the hospital authorities allowed appeal days around the wards, which Nick publicized on the hospital radio, the children in Paediatrics ransacked toy cupboards and bookshelves, the women in Obstetrics offered excess baby clothes, hundreds of hospital visitors emptied their pockets and purses into Nikki's big red appeal buckets, and Jan even found enough courage to speak out in public.

Katie fixed an interview on local radio for Jan, then took him by the hand and made sure he went through with it. Well, it was only five minutes on a Tuesday afternoon and hardly anyone would be listening, he thought. Then he discovered that Karen had taped the programme and was hiring it out at a pound a time! "Every little helps," she'd said, grinning like a little cat.

And every little had certainly helped. Here he was, part of a three-vehicle convoy filled with supplies – and Christmas presents – for the refugees back home.

Jan Buczowski tapped his fingers on the dashboard, rhythmically, 6/8 time, and hummed an old Slavonic tune that Granya used to sing to him.

"That's nice," Serena Robinson nodded her head in time to the music. "What is it?"

“A song for a special feast day,” Jan explained. “Granya used to sing it at the dark end of winter, just as spring began.”

Serena Robinson smiled. “Very apt,” she said.

“Apt? What is that?” Jan reached in his pocket for his notebook.

“Suitable,” Serena explained. “A suitable song for coming out of the dark days into the light.” She smiled at him briefly, knowingly. “What’s it called?” she asked.

Jan grinned and answered her in Serbo-Croat.

“Don’t be daft, Jan,” Serena laughed. “Tell me in English.”

Jan thought for a moment, searching for the most apt words. Then a wide grin spread across his face. “Saint Agatha’s Blessing,” he said.

Follow six student nurses as they come to terms with doctors, patients, study ... and each other.

Bette Paul

1: Katie Goes to College

Katie wants to get involved in *everything* when she starts at nursing college. But has she bitten off more than she can chew?

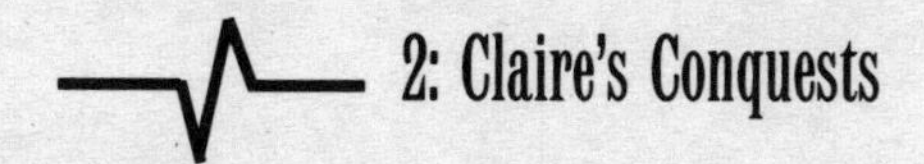

2: Claire's Conquests

Claire's finding nursing harder than she expected. And she's having problems with her love-life, too...

Look out for:

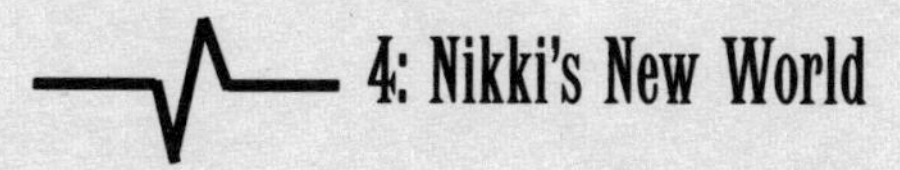

4: Nikki's New World

Nikki feels worlds apart from her patients in the rough Brassington estates. But maybe they have more in common than she realizes...

All the thrills of a busy Emergency Room, from the ever-popular Caroline B. Cooney.

EMERGENCY ROOM

CITY HOSPITAL. EMERGENCY ROOM. And the evening has only just begun...

6.00 p.m. Volunteers Diana and Seth arrive – eager to help save lives...

6.38 p.m. Emergency – gun shot wound – victim of a deadly drug battle...

6.55 p.m. Suspected cardiac in Bed 8. Another routine heart attack? Not for Diana...

7.16 p.m. All systems go – Alec, sixteen, clings to life by a thread.

This is the Emergency Room. Precious seconds are ticking away, and Diana and Seth hold the balance between life and death...

•PATSY KELLY• INVESTIGATES

When Patsy starts work at her uncle's detective agency, her instructions are very clear. Do the filing. Answer the phone. Make the tea. *Don't* get involved in any of the cases.

But somehow Patsy can't help getting involved...

And it's not just the cases she has to worry about. There's Billy, too. Will she ever work out what she *really* feels about him...?

•PATSY KELLY• INVESTIGATES

Anne Cassidy

Available now:
A Family Affair
End of the Line

Look out for:
No Through Road

Point Romance

Look out for this heartwarming Point Romance mini series:

First Comes Love

by Jennifer Baker

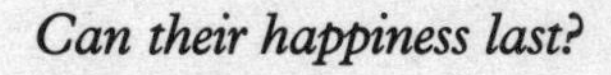

Can their happiness last?

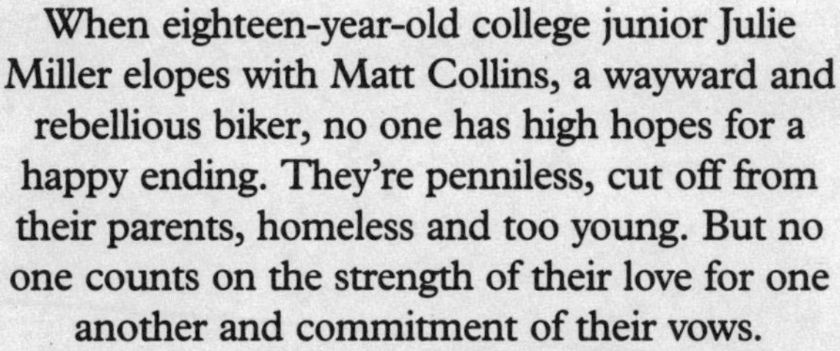

When eighteen-year-old college junior Julie Miller elopes with Matt Collins, a wayward and rebellious biker, no one has high hopes for a happy ending. They're penniless, cut off from their parents, homeless and too young. But no one counts on the strength of their love for one another and commitment of their vows.

Four novels, *To Have and To Hold, For Better For Worse, In Sickness and in Health,* and *Till Death Do Us Part*, follow Matt and Julie through their first year of marriage.

Once the honeymoon is over, they have to deal with the realities of life. Money worries, tensions, jealousies, illness, accidents, and the most heartbreaking decision of their lives.

Can their love survive?

Four novels to touch your heart . . .